This book is a work of fiction. The names, characters, places, and incidents are products of the writer's imagination or have been used fictitiously and are not to be construed as real. Any resemblance to persons, living or dead, actual events, locale, or organizations is entirely coincidental.

D1617020

Revenge sex and a healthy dose of a bad boy making all the wrong decisions equals one hell of a wild ride. Horse optional.

Zayden Moon and his brothers are back home for the old man's funeral, but too bad none of them give a damn what happens to the failing ranch they've inherited or all the bad memories that come with it. Now Zayden has more than his murky past and the ranch to contend with. As usual, trouble comes searching for him when he's asked to rescue a woman lost on the mountain, stranded on Valentines' Day of all things, and he's the only man who knows where to look. And whoooeee, there's a lot to look at when it comes to this curvaceous beauty.

Esme thought she was going to the mountain getaway to receive a diamond ring, and instead she's abandoned by her boyfriend and left to make her own way down the jagged terrain. When a sexy cowboy rides in on a white steed, she thinks she's seeing things, but soon his warm, rough hands show her otherwise. A hot and heavy dose of revenge sex seems to be in order too, right?

If Zayden had a heart, he'd be falling for the woman with spunk to match her wild curls, but he knows better than to attempt a relationship. And Lordy, Esme sure gravitates to the worst men... except there's something more to Zayden than he allows anyone to see. If she ever figures out what, she might give Zayden a chance, because the man's kisses sure can knot a woman up.

The Moon Ranch Series:
TOUGH AND TAMED
SCREWED AND SATISFIED
CHISELED AND CHERISHED

TOUGH AND TAMED

BY

Em Petrova

Chapter One

The whoop of a siren brought Zayden's gaze to the rearview mirror, and he groaned. He hadn't been in the county for three minutes and he was already getting nailed by the cops.

Lights flashed in his rearview mirror, and he eased his old Chevy to the side of the road, racking his brain for any laws he may have violated. Speeding? No.

Not a drop of alcohol passed his lips in months either, and his driving had been steady, with his sights set on the big mountain range in the distance.

Annoyed and not minding one bit if he was being an asshole, he didn't bother to roll down his window for the approaching deputy. When the uniformed man's body filled the entire window, Zayden just stared back at him.

He rapped on the glass. "Roll it down."

With a snort, he did, and a fresh gust of mountain air hit his face, bringing more than clear-headedness—it brought a hell of a lot of memories rushing in. The scents of pine mixed with snow made him think of his father. And damn if he'd give that son-of-a-bitch any more consideration than he deserved.

"License, registration and proof of insurance," the deputy said.

Zayden leaned across the console and popped the glove compartment. He pulled out his information and passed it to the familiar-looking lawman before digging in his back pocket for his wallet and driver's license.

"Don't I remember you from Stokes High?" Zayden asked.

"That's right, Moon."

Zayden squinted an eye at him. "Heard you were a deputy. Thought you'd have a better job by now, Dickies." The old nickname rolled off his tongue.

The high school jock who'd lived to give Zayden and his two younger brothers hell every chance he got leveled a glare at him. For a moment, he just bore the deputy-on-a-power-trip's scrutiny.

"You'll never change, will ya, Moon?"

"And you'll never stop being a dick. Why did you pull me over? Recognize the truck and remembered you hadn't gotten your quota of intimidation in for the day?"

Dickies stared at his license and back to Zayden's face as if he handed over a fake ID and was lying about his age. But both he and Dickies sported more lines of age, his maybe more from the life he'd led the past decade since high school.

2

"You don't have anything to say, do you? Because I didn't violate any laws," he pressed.

"Get outta the truck, Moon."

Zayden made a little shooing motion for him to step away from the door so he could open it. When he stepped out and unfolded to his full height, a hefty six inches over Dickie's penis-shaped head, he took a moment to use his size to intimidate instead of a badge.

"Well?" Zayden asked.

"Step to the back. There's something that requires your attention." Dickies took off to the rear of the truck and pointed to the mud-and-road-salt-splattered tailgate.

"Are you gonna give me hell because the tailgate's a different color than the rest of the truck? You got somethin' against blue?" He'd gotten rear-ended back in Nevada some years back and replaced the tailgate, but never got around to painting it to match the rest of the white truck.

"No, this is the problem." He pointed. "I can't see your license plate number. You realize it's the driver's obligation to keep the plate clean at all times, right?"

The Moon temper rose up in him, and he eyed the filthy plate. Yeah, the letters and numbers couldn't be seen through the grime, and Dickies was being a jackass. Some things never changed. All Zayden wanted to do was get home and end this hell of being back in Stokes after so many years.

3

He knew just how to clean the plate.

Stepping up to the back of the truck, he squared his hips, planted his feet... and unzipped his fly.

"What the hell are you doing?" Dickies ground out.

"Quiet or it'll crawl back up." He focused hard, and the spurt of piss left his body. He aimed the stream at the plate, splashing upward to wash away the filth.

Dickies sent him a glare that might make other men wither, but Zayden wasn't other men.

He stuffed his cock back into his boxers and zipped up with a little flick of his wrist. Turning to Dickies, he said, "There. Now you can read it."

"Get back into your truck, Moon," he grated between clenched teeth.

With a tug on the brim of his Stetson, he sauntered to the truck and climbed behind the wheel, while Dickies returned to his cruiser to look up the plate or maybe jerk his meat.

He glanced back, and as soon as Dickies got out of his car, Zayden rolled up his window again.

This time when Dickies rapped on the glass, he put some force behind it.

"Can I help you, Deputy Dickies?"

"Dickinson," he bit off. "You've got a string of prior arrests, Moon."

"That so?"

4

"Bar fights. You broke a man's nose."

"Who hasn't?" he drawled.

"You were arrested for using excessive force against a coworker at a construction company in Nevada."

"Yeah, that wasn't the best idea. I shouldn't have gotten caught for that one. Moral of the story is always hide your weapons after a fight."

"There are other incidents on your record."

"So? Am I breaking the law now?"

Dickies handed him a piece of paper, and it flapped in the wind. For a moment, Zayden considered letting the air rip it from his fingers so Dickies would be forced to write up another, but in the end, he figured he'd fucked with the man enough for one day and took it.

Public urination. Fine of $250 plus community service.

Deputies didn't hand out community service citations—he was using his power of authority to screw with him.

"Motherfucker. You always were a real dick." He crumpled the citation in his fist and tossed it onto the floor.

"Don't forget to pay that or see the magistrate to be assigned that community service."

Zayden settled his gaze on the asshole until Dickies' face mottled red. "You make a great welcoming committee, Dickies. Stokes, Colorado is in your debt." His sarcasm had the old rival's face growing redder with suppressed rage.

"Sorry to hear about your dad, Moon."

Zayden grunted and reached for the button to roll up his window. "I'm not." He started the truck and pulled away, leaving Dickies standing on the side of the road without the last word.

It didn't make him feel any better to have gotten it, though. Now he had a nice fine and community service he probably wouldn't stick around long enough to do. He was only here to see his father's casket lowered into the ground, and then he'd hit the highway once more, heading far away from this Podunk town and all its horrible memories.

As he drove, some of them flooded back. Dear old dad passed out on the front lawn—again. Zayden closing the door and locking it for the night, telling his brothers Dane and Asher to let their dad lie there. But by morning, he'd always wake to find Chaz Moon passed out on the sagging couch in the living room, set up with a garbage can near his head in case he needed to puke, and Zayden knew it was Asher's doing.

His kid brother never could stand to see their dad in his drunken state. He was the son who removed Chaz's boots and hat and put a pillow beneath his head.

Well now nobody needed to help out their whiskey-soaked old man—he'd drank himself into an early grave, and good fucking riddance to the piece of shit.

"Screw this," Zayden said for the millionth time of his life.

He could turn around, let the son of a bitch be buried without his sons at his side. When had he ever given a crap about any of them? Zayden made sure his brothers had food in their bellies and caught the school bus in the mornings. He'd dropped out of high school at sixteen to try to keep the ranch afloat.

The ranch... He didn't quite know how to feel about the place. It presented a bog of bad memories — of getting backhanded across the face and nursing a swollen and bleeding lip too many times to count. Of too little money. Christ, there never was enough of that.

But there were good things about the ranch too. His brothers' antics always kept him laughing. And the horses and the faded blue of the mountains looming in the distance. How the sky looked before a snow — an icy cold blue like it appeared right now.

Storm's a-comin', and he'd be meeting it head on.

He stopped at the turn for the driveway, just idling in the middle of the road, staring at the familiar rusted mailbox and pitted drive.

When he'd left a decade ago, he'd sworn he'd never come back. Now here he was, dragged back by a phone call from Mimi.

The older woman stayed on at the ranch, and Lord knew why. She'd always been a saint, but living a life in the service of Chaz Moon made her into more of a masochist in his eyes.

She lived just at the end of this driveway, and she'd be happy to see him.

And his father was dead.

Zayden took the turn and bumped toward the ranch. The fields lay dormant beneath the layer of snow. They ran right up to the Ute Indian lands beyond the borders of the Moon Ranch, as peaceful as ever.

To the opposite side was a copse of pines that bordered a creek where he and his brothers would fly fish in summers. But the older Zayden got, the less he had time to fish. He was too busy picking up the shattered pieces of their lives.

The fencing looked dilapidated, completely missing in areas, like teeth punched out. He stuck his tongue into a space in his own mouth where he'd lost a molar in a fistfight a few years back.

The barn needed work — the roof replaced and the gaps closed with new boards. Were there even horses here anymore? He didn't see a single head of cattle in the fields between the barn and mountains.

When he finally forced himself to look at the house, his chest burned. Too many emotions to process flooded in, and he braked hard. Slamming the truck into park, he got out and kicked the door shut.

Then he tore off his hat and stood glaring at the place. Last thing he wanted to do was stick around here, but the old feelings of obligation, of being the glue, the fixer, the guy in charge, had him turning circles in the driveway to see all that needed done on the place.

His father was dead. He and his brothers would inherit the land, that was if the old man didn't owe every acre to the Jack Daniels distillery and the cowboy bar down the road.

He shoved his hat back on his head and started toward the house. Before he reached it, the door opened and a woman stepped out. She looked much older, hair completely white, and her shoulders slumped. She wore a cardigan that swallowed up her tiny frame, but he knew the blue would be the same color as her eyes.

As she watched him cross the yard, a smile spread over her face. "Zayden, my boy." She opened her arms, and he mounted the porch to step up to her.

He slipped his arms around her and lifted her off her feet.

"Put me down! I'm old and I'll break!" She squealed like a much younger woman.

He gave her a gentle squeeze and set her down. Looking into her eyes, he said, "He's really dead?"

She nodded.

"Thank Christ."

She didn't give him a disapproving look—she knew what he and his brothers had endured at the hands of their father.

"Come inside. I've got supper warming in the oven."

He sniffed the air, and through the open doorway detected the scents of roast chicken and buttery biscuits. His stomach growled. "Never understood how you managed to make such good meals on so little. And I imagine it only got worse after we all left."

She shook her head. "Time to put all that behind ya now, boy. Come in. We're letting all the heat out."

February took a lot of firewood to heat the house, which he knew from personal experience. He could almost feel the weight of the ax in his hand and the strain of his muscles after hours of chopping daily just to keep them warm.

He entered the house and shut the door behind him. He stood there, looking around at the furniture that needed dragged outside and lit with a match. The worn carpets, faded curtains. But everything remained clean—Mimi saw to that.

"Why did you stay, Mimi?"

She turned those pale blue eyes up to him. "You asked me to."

"But that was years and years ago."

"Yes, but in my family, you make a promise and see it out."

"You can go now, Mimi. I release you."

"We'll see about that." She eyed him.

He opened his mouth to say more, but the door flew open behind them.

Zayden turned to see his youngest brother Asher. Taller, packed with muscle from doing whatever he'd been doing, wherever he'd been doing it.

Their gazes met, and a grin split Asher's features. "The drunk old rotter finally keeled over, huh?"

Zayden burst out laughing for the first time in… well, he couldn't recall when he'd last found amusement in anything. He strode forward. "Damn, it's good to see your face." He hugged Asher, and his baby brother thumped him hard on the back.

"Where's Dane?" he asked as he pulled back.

"Who the hell knows. Strippin'?"

"He says he's a male dancer."

"Is that any different?" Zayden and Asher locked gazes again and shared another laugh.

"Hell if I know if it's different. He's married to a stripper too." Asher turned to Mimi. "Honey, I smelled those biscuits from a mile down the road. Gimme a hug and then let me at 'em."

Zayden followed them into the kitchen and watched Mimi place things from the oven onto the table while he and Asher found things to tease each other about.

It was like old times.

11

God, don't let it be like old times.

* * * * *

Zayden had no idea how the Moon Ranch was still in operation.

No money and no ranch hands left. The place needed updates to the outbuildings, the fence and so much more, and every dime died along with their father.

A handful of cattle seemed content enough in their winter pasture, and someone had given them a round bale and some winter feeds. The solar-powered wells kept them watered.

But how the hell did a ranch that barely scraped by with him and his brothers working their asses off ever scrape by in such a neglected state now?

His father had a pension from the Army, but he drank it all up. Always had, which was why the responsibility fell on Zayden's shoulders.

He drifted into the barn. The space looked relatively clean and the stalls contained fresh hay. The few horses left looked cared for, and whoever still came to help out was either devoted or dumb as a rock.

Zayden was far from stupid, though. This must be Mimi's doing. In some way, she'd managed to hire someone, probably using her own money.

He closed the barn door and headed to the house. With the funeral scheduled for later in the week, he had a bit of time to figure things out. First, he and Mimi needed to have a good, honest chat.

When he reached the front porch, the boards sagged beneath his weight. On the old man's favorite chair in the corner, Asher sat staring across the land.

As Zayden approached, his brother looked up. "Spent the last seven years of my life tryin' to avoid this place," he said.

"Know the feeling."

"Dane still ain't here." Asher nudged the brim of his hat back and looked at Zayden.

He felt that old stirring — to do something, to take charge. "I'll call him now." He added that to his growing mental list of things to do. Talk to Mimi. Find out if there really was any money left. See how fast they could sell the ranch.

"Z."

He turned at Asher's voice. "Yeah?"

He and his youngest brother had the same eyes as their mother, which according to dear old pops, gave more than enough reason to knock them around more than Dane, who resembled him most. The curse of looking like their mother, who'd been smart enough to split but cruel enough to leave her three sons at the mercy of a drunk, always bound him and Asher.

"What's gonna happen with this place?" Asher rubbed at his nose, which sported a new bump from being broken at some point in the past few years.

"Dunno. What do you think we should do with it?"

Asher snorted. "You always took care o' things. I have no damn idea."

Yeah, it felt like a boulder on his shoulders. Nothing new there.

He walked into the house and hadn't even moved to close the door before Mimi's voice rang out. "Shut the door!"

"I know, I'm letting all the heat out," he called back.

She popped her head out of the kitchen, a smile on her face. "You boys."

"We're men now. Men who know how to shut a door." He did so now.

"I guess it's an old habit to tell ya off. One I missed, if I'm honest."

"Tellin' us off was something you've missed?" He couldn't help but smile back at her.

"When you've spent as many years as I have basically alone here, then you miss the oddest things. Want some coffee, do ya?"

"Sounds great." He didn't bother removing his boots as he moved to the kitchen table. Mimi put a mug of black, rich coffee before him. He looked up. "How do you know I still take it black?"

"Been drinkin' black coffee since you were thirteen. Now what's on your mind? I saw you walking the ranch." She poured herself a mug with an

14

owl on it. The woman loved owls, and he and his brothers had carved her small owls from sticks for Christmas or birthdays. He twisted in his seat to see the row of small wooden objects still lined up on the windowsill.

"How did you do it, Mimi? How did you keep living here after we'd gone?"

"It's easy when you just think of the work you put into each day." She took a sip.

He felt huge sitting beside her. "How old are you now?"

She gasped in shock and drew up straight. "You never ask a lady her age. Have you learned nothing of the world, Zayden?"

He chuckled. "Guess not. So you're eighty?"

She slapped him. "I just might dump this hot coffee right on your crotch for that one, boy. I'm seventy."

"Ah, quite young then. My apologies." He sipped the coffee, finding it just as good as always. Everything Mimi made tasted better. Or maybe it was just the care she put into every morsel—something all three Moon boys had ached for.

She nudged a plate of cinnamon buns across the table, and he took one in hand. Even the plate brought back memories, because it was one of a set that had all been smashed by their father in some drunken state or other. Either he was pathetic drunk

Chaz, falling over himself and breaking shit, or he was enraged drunk Chaz.

He shook off the thought and bit into the roll. After he chewed the delicious cinnamon sweetness, he met Mimi's gaze. She was like their momma and grandmother all rolled into one. No one knew them better.

"You're thinking of selling the ranch, aren't you, Zayden?"

He nodded. "Who's been coming to help out with the animals?"

"My great-nephew from the rez." Mimi was part Ute, and her blue eyes came from her mother, who'd taken her away at a young age. But she'd returned to her people later in life, and lived there until a desperate young boy had run into their village and begged for help.

Without looking back, Mimi came with Zayden, and spent her days here on the Moon Ranch. Too many days.

"Who's paying your great-nephew?" he asked.

"I do what I can to help him when he needs it. He's got young'uns who need babysitting, and I go up there sometimes."

"Good trade." He sighed. "I think I've gotta sell the ranch, Mimi."

Her name wasn't Mimi, but Asher had dubbed her that at the age of ten. Her Native American name was Chipeta, which meant White Singing Bird. But

16

her mother had called her Barbara. Neither fit her as well as Mimi.

She wore that crease between her brows, which appeared when she disapproved of one of her 'boys' as she called them.

"Say it plain, Mimi."

"Our ancestors said not to waste good land. This is good land. You can build it into something, Zayden. You and your brothers can make Moon Ranch what it always longed to be."

Yeah... right. If not for the drunk owner. If not for the dysfunction and emotional abuse, and never mention the split lips.

"I think I'm going to take one of the horses out this morning and see more of the ranch," he heard himself say.

Pick up the pieces. Do what is right for the ranch. Wasn't that always his motto? He didn't want to fall back into old habits, but he couldn't ignore Mimi's words either.

She nodded, a trace of happiness in her eyes. "You should take the white gelding. He gets restless if he isn't ridden, according to my great-nephew."

"I will. Don't let Asher eat all those cinnamon rolls, and if Dane ever shows up, he doesn't deserve one."

She drew the plate in front of herself. "Maybe I'll eat them all."

He flashed a grin. "You could use some fat on those bones. I'll be back this afternoon."

* * * * *

After riding the perimeter of the ranch and mentally noting all that needed tended to, Zayden tucked the white horse up in the barn with some fresh hay. The winter afternoon daylight faded fast, and the lights in the house glowed like yellow butter on the snow.

He looked around for a sign of another truck parked in the driveway but saw none. Dane never came, and Asher apparently left.

A kernel of anger that always seemed to live in his gut blossomed and spread. He stalked inside and found Mimi rolling out cookie dough on the kitchen counter.

"Dane's not here," he said.

"No."

"Asher left."

"Went down to the bar." Her tone sounded sad, and no wonder. Alcoholism ran in families, and Zayden had done his damnedest to avoid the places as a result. Who knew what Asher was up to, but he'd find out sooner or later. Hopefully not after his brother did something stupid.

He crossed the kitchen and whipped open the cupboard above the fridge. Bottles of whiskey crowded the depths. With a growl of rage, he grabbed the trash can and started ripping bottles down from the cupboard. He dropped each with a hard clink, until the top bottles smashed.

After he had them all, he picked up the can, he stormed through the rest of the house, to all of his dad's old hiding places, and tossed every last bottle. When the can grew full, he yanked out the bag and replaced it. By the time he finished, there were three bags on the front porch.

After his purging fit, he went into the kitchen and found the coffeepot hot. He drank half a mug before he looked to Mimi. "Think I'll head into town and buy feed before the store closes for the day."

"You should. We're getting low," Mimi said.

He drained his mug and set it into the empty sink. "Be back in time for supper."

"I've got a casserole in the oven."

He looked at the baked cookies on the counter in the shape of hearts and sprinkled with white sugar. He cocked a brow. "Hearts?"

"It's Valentine's Day, Zayden. Did you forget?"

"Guess so." He planted a kiss on her cheek. "Got to kiss my sweetheart, though."

She grinned broadly and waved him away. "Always the charmer. Hurry to town after the feed. That storm on the mountain's headed this way."

Chapter Two

Killer lace teddy—check. Thigh-high stockings—check.

Esme turned to the mirror and fluffed her wild curls around her face. The brown ringlets had a way of adding a sex appeal all of their own, and Owen loved to grab her hair and—

She nibbled her lower lip in anticipation. When he'd invited her on a weekend getaway, she'd been excited. But the moment she heard it was for Valentine's Day, well, her mind went *there*...

To the diamond ring every woman dreamed of receiving on the holiday designed for lovers.

The quaint cabin on the mountain added a nice touch, she had to admit. Owen knew she loved all things outdoorsy, and that was exactly why, when he dropped to bended knee and popped the question, she would say yes.

A flurry of nerves hit.

He waited for her just beyond this bathroom door, and she was stalling.

No, not stalling—letting the excitement build.

She leaned close to the bathroom mirror again and inspected her lipstick, swiping a smudge at one corner. After checking her teeth to make sure there wasn't any red lipstick on them, she drew in a shaky breath.

"Showtime."

She quietly opened the bathroom door and stuck one stockinged toe into the bedroom where Owen waited for her. She extended her leg, hooking it around the doorjamb. Then she slipped out a hip, which she wiggled to show off the sheer lace and the curve of her buttocks.

Not a sound could be heard—Owen was probably stunned speechless, and that would mean she'd achieved her goal of dolling up for the special moment.

When she popped out into the room, locking her gaze on the bed where she knew he'd be, a harsh gasp left her lips.

He wasn't on the bed.

Or in any of the corners either.

Well, her little seductive ploy wasn't spoiled, because she could find him in the kitchen. They'd never had kitchen table sex… or any sex besides in a bed, for that matter. But who cared? Tonight was *the night*.

She sashayed through the rustic cabin, swinging her hips and walking as if she was on a catwalk.

Brushing her curls back over her shoulders, she cooed, "Oh Owennnn."

No sound came in response.

With a bit of annoyance, she dropped the act and entered the living room, one hand on her hip.

The space sat empty. Spinning, she looked at the small oak kitchen, and Owen wasn't standing there either.

"What the hell?" she said to the empty space. "Owen?"

She walked to the front door and whipped it open. It was just like him to be waiting outside—he knew how much she loved the outdoors, and a proposal in the winter wonderland of the mountain was beyond perfect.

A shiver hit her skin as the wintry wind blew at her face. She blinked away some snowflakes and stared around her. Snow piled up, and it came down in those big fat flakes that Colorado was known for.

"Owen!" She peered toward the parking area to the side of the wood cabin. Her stomach dipped low and quick—like she sat on a rollercoaster and just took a curve at high speed.

No Jeep. No Owen.

Maybe he'd gone down the mountain to town, had forgotten something. Flowers? Champagne?

She hurriedly closed the door and wrapped her arms around her scantily-clad body. If he'd gone to town, it would take a good hour. The drive up the mountain, navigating the switch-backed roads, took some time. Nothing for Esme to do but settle in and wait.

She felt silly sitting around in the teddy and stockings, so she marched to the bedroom, reached for her bathrobe—and froze with one hand on the fuzzy robe.

Where the fuck was Owen's bag?

Shock hit her square in the face. There had to be a mistake—he wouldn't just up and leave.

Would he?

Her mind rushed over their ride here, the night they'd spent in each other's arms... and the dead silence between them.

She searched her memory of his handsome face and could recall no smiles. In fact, he'd looked a bit unhappy, if she was honest with herself.

Maybe something is wrong, something he didn't want to worry me with. He had to rush off.

But what could be so urgent that he couldn't call out to her in the bathroom before leaving?

Pissed, she ran to the front door again and threw it open. Wind and snow hit her mostly-bare body, and she rasped at the cold before slamming the door once more.

He wasn't here. He might not return.

He may not propose.

Running back to the bedroom, she grabbed her cell off the nightstand, but before she even glanced at the screen, she knew she had no service. The mountain was a dead zone, and she couldn't call Owen and ask him what was going on.

Dread slithered low in her belly. *I can't even call for help, and I have no way down the mountain.*

The son of a bitch had left her stranded, wearing nothing but a scrap of lace and a trace of perfume on her wrists and the insides of her dang thighs. Her neglected thighs, she might add. Right now, he was supposed to be rubbing his delicious beard all over her goosebumped skin, and instead, he'd stranded her.

Fury slammed her like a glacier. She threw her cell phone down on the mattress and balled her fists. "Damn you, Owen Walden. I'm going to punch you in the throat first chance I get."

How did she plan to do that, when she was stuck here on the mountain, alone in a cabin in the middle of nowhere, and with a winter storm upon her?

She had little choice but to head down the mountain on foot as quickly as possible. The lower elevations would have better weather, and she'd probably have cell service too.

Good thing she was an experienced hiker.

She stripped off the stockings and lace, tossing all into her bag. She hadn't planned to do much hiking while on the mountain. Her plans had included more time spent on her back with her legs in the air than in a parka and boots.

Damn him. Damn, damn, damn.

Gaining what calm she could muster, she dressed in layers of thermal underwear, T-shirt and flannel overtop. On her bottom, more thermal and jeans, because it was all she had with her. Thank goodness for thick socks and good boots.

Looking at her overcoat, she wished she'd been better prepared. But who packed to be stranded on a snow-covered mountain in the middle of February after her boyfriend left her high and dry?

Bastard. She twisted her lips and zipped her bag shut with a violent flick of her wrist. The zipper caught on the teddy and wouldn't budge. She spent five angry minutes cussing and battling the lace from the zipper teeth before managing to close her bag.

She donned her coat, canvas but too lightweight to be called a winter jacket, slung her bag over her body and went to the front door again.

With a last look at the cozy cabin, she said, "I don't ever want to set eyes on you again," and didn't know if she was talking to the cabin or the man who'd abandoned her in it.

Once she reached the road leading down the mountain, she realized she might have made a poor decision. But heading back to the cabin was a lost cause. Without the ability to call for help and left without a set of wheels, what choice did she have?

Winter storms could leave her stranded in the cabin for days. Her only hope rested on reaching a lower elevation and place a call.

To whom? She didn't have family in the area, having moved to Boulder for a position in the credit union. And her friends were short on the ground. She did have a few people she talked to at work, other bank tellers, but would any be willing to brave the roads to get her?

She groaned. What choice did she have but to reach a place where she could call for help? That was what humans did — lent each other a helping hand — and she would just have to suck it up and ask despite her independence.

The first leg of the road was relatively easy walking, though by the time she reached the next switchback, her shoulder ached from the weight of her bag. With a scowl, she thought she could toss out the useless lingerie, but it wouldn't lighten the load.

She shifted the bag to the other shoulder and continued on the next jaunt. Snow caught on her eyelashes, and she blinked to dispel them. They came back again and again, the white world fragmented in the wetness, and she swiped a gloved hand over them.

Her curls exploded from under her knit hat, but at least her hair wasn't blown across her face by the evil wind.

By the time she reached the next sharp angle of the road, her lungs burned from the cold, and her toes grew chilled too. The thick socks weren't doing much to keep the tips warm, and her gloves weren't rated for lower temperatures.

Who knew she'd be mountaineering in a snowstorm instead of curled up in her lover's arms by the log fire, with her brand-new diamond glittering on her finger?

No, this wasn't a snowstorm—snow didn't feel like knives hitting her skin.

The shards of ice began to pelt her face. Each ball that struck her shoulders sounded like BBs fired at her. She squinted into the now raging monster of the storm, and the snow that had turned to ice quickly turned to freezing rain.

Drizzle enveloped her in a cloud, and it didn't take long to realize she was in over her head. If she stayed out in this rain, she'd be soaked and hypothermic. She had two choices—up or down.

She checked her cell for the tenth time and still no bars in sight. Some very dirty words exploded from her lips, and she trudged on, through the soaking rain. By the next switchback, she discovered her boots were not as waterproof as they had claimed on the box back in the store. Her canvas coat was soaked at the shoulders and weighing her down.

For a moment, she considered dropping her heavy bag and leaving it here on the mountain, but her survival skills kicked in. She may need the extra layers and if all else failed, she could wrap the lace teddy around a tree limb and set it on fire to keep warm.

Please let there be a snowmobiler out. Please let someone come by.

It better not be Owen. At this point, if she saw the man she'd probably knock him unconscious and leave him for dead.

She quickened her pace, but what felt like an hour later, she still had no service and felt no lower in elevation. How long was this road? She'd been so wrapped up with Owen while they drove to the cabin, stealing looks at him from beneath her lashes, excitement warm in her belly. Now, the only warmth she possessed resembled a blaze of anger.

The rain lightened, but then the wind picked up to a howling gale, cutting through her wet coat and boots and freezing her exposed face. With a cry, she searched the roadside for a sign of shelter. Another cabin, or hell, at this point, she'd take a house belonging to a troll as long as it was dry and out of this dangerous wind.

When she began shaking from cold, she took that as a good sign. She was still able to generate some body heat, but for how long?

She spotted a fallen pine, the heavy branches bowed under the weight of snow. She'd once read an article about a man who'd built a shelter from pine limbs, and he'd been sheltered enough to make it through a storm. Thank God for her research about Colorado winters before making the move from Tennessee.

Looking from the road to the tree and back again, she weighed her options. *Think, Esme.* But all she

28

could think about was how cold she was, and her brain didn't fire like normal.

She could sit under the branches for a little while and attempt to warm herself a bit. That was smartest, right?

Climbing the bank took some effort, but she finally mounted the higher ground. Crouching, she ducked under the branches and scooted her back against the trunk. The sharp tang of pine and cold snow burned her nostrils, and she raised a wet glove to pinch her nose. She could scarcely feel the tip, she was so frozen.

She unzipped the collar of her coat and buried as much of her face inside as she could. Then she stuck her gloved hands under her arms and drew her knees up to her chest to conserve heat.

The wind raged on like a wild animal, and after a while, she felt like howling with it. What good would it do, though, when she needed her energy and the man she wanted to release her tirade on was nowhere around?

What if Owen had gone back to the cabin and found her gone?

Dammit, walking back would take hours, and no way could she climb the mountain in her state of fatigue. She had to stick to her plan. Head down the mountain. Find a spot of cell service and call Natalie from the bank for a ride.

Slightly warmer, her morale began to rise again, when the rain returned. As fresh drops cut through the thick needles of the pine and trickled onto her neck, she felt the first true fear strike her heart.

Maybe she would never get down this mountain.

On the heels of that came a cheery thought. *At least Owen will be charged with murder.*

* * * * *

"My eyes must be failing. I swear I'm lookin' at one of the Moon boys over there."

The feed store owner's voice reached Zayden all the way down the aisle, and he pivoted to eye the old timer.

"I am a Moon." He slowly approached the checkout counter.

The owner stared. "Tell me your brothers aren't with ya."

"No, why?"

"Because where there are three Moons, there's a parole officer."

"C'mon, Travis. None of us ever shoplifted from your store."

"No, that was your daddy. Oh damn. I don't mean to be insensitive. I'm sorry about his passing."

With a shake of his head, Zayden chuckled. "I'm not." He set a couple items on the counter and nodded toward the stacks of feed. "I need a couple bags plus this."

Travis rang him up and then peered through his squared bifocals. "$42.92."

Zayden grunted and peeled off a couple bills. "Your prices have gone up since I was in here last."

"That was a good decade ago, Moon. Which one are you, by the way?"

Amusement twitched the corner of his lips. "Zayden."

"That's right. You were in school with my granddaughter, but you dropped out and didn't graduate with her."

"That's me." He picked up the bag and moved to the feed. Being back in a small town like Stokes, and known by everyone, wasn't giving him any warm, fuzzy feelings.

He tossed one bag of feed over his shoulder, went to the truck, and dropped it into the bed. Then he turned back for the second bag.

When he got inside, Travis and another older man in coveralls were standing around, shooting the breeze. He caught snippets of their conversation as he hefted the next bag of feed.

"Missing?" Travis' raised voice carried to him.

"That's the tale. A sad one too. She's lost on the mountain."

"In the middle of that squall? God, it's gotta be comin' down around her ears by now."

The other man nodded. "Guess her boyfriend called it in."

"Foul play?"

The man shrugged. "There's a search party going out in half hour."

Zayden lowered the bag to the stack again and turned to them. "How old is the woman?"

"Dunno. Grown but still young enough. I heard a rumor at the credit union that she'd gone on a retreat with her boyfriend for Valentine's Day, but I ain't sure about that."

"Damn, that's rough." Zayden picked up the bag again.

"Not many know that mountain," Travis said.

He stopped in his tracks. He knew if he turned to the men, they'd be staring at him.

"You know that mountain, Moon," he said.

Zayden grunted and shot him a glance. Sure enough, they were both looking at him expectantly.

"No one knows that mountain like you do, Zayden."

Dammit, they were dumping more on his shoulders, and the floundering ranch and his father's death were enough.

"You might be her only chance," Travis added.

Hell.

He couldn't walk away from that truth.

Hoisting the bag over his shoulder again, he said, "Tell them I'm in. But I'm going up solo."

One of the men let out a cheer, and he didn't look back to see who. He dumped the other bag into the truck and closed the tailgate. Then he jumped behind the wheel and looked out at the mountain.

It appeared whited out, the top completely invisible. If there was a woman up there, she didn't have long. He needed more particulars before he headed home for his gear. He drove down the street a ways.

When he pulled into the fire station, the chief and a few other men were in the parking lot, scrambling their search party.

Zayden got out and started toward them. The chief looked up and groaned loudly. "You set fire to something up on that ranch o' yours, Moon? Because we got better things to do than put out a blaze."

God, he hated this town.

"I'm joining the search. Where was she last seen?"

"One of the cabins owned by Raedke. You know them?"

He gave a hard nod. "Which cabin?"

"The upper one."

"Why the hell is there even access to that cabin this time of year? Nobody should be on that mountain."

"I agree, but take it up with Raedke."

33

They all knew that idiot was out for a buck and didn't give a crap about safety. Besides some mountain cabins he rented to tourists, he owned a trailer park and a few rental units known for unsafe conditions such as gas leaks.

"I'll head up there now." Zayden turned for the truck. The chief called out for him to wait, but he ignored him and drove away.

At the road to the mountain, he paused to put chains on his tires. The long, snow-covered road took ages to navigate, and he could do better if he had a snowmobile, but any big boy toys owned by the Moons had long since been traded for whiskey, if they had ever existed.

When he reached the flatter part of the mountain where the cabin was located, the snow piled in deep drifts along the wooden walls. Not a tire track could be seen. Footprint either, for that matter.

He jumped out of the truck and ran to the door. The place wasn't locked, and he quickly scoured the cabin, finding nothing but a rumpled bed and a towel drying on a bar in the bathroom.

She wasn't here, and hadn't been for some time. The best he could do was head back down and hope to spot her or a track leading to her.

Who the hell was this woman? Clearly a dumb one, if she had risked the mountain cabin in February. Colorado weather was unpredictable at this time of year, at best. And deadly at worst. He'd known plenty of hikers who succumbed to the elements in the dead of summer, let alone in a storm.

As he started down the mountain, he passed two snowmobiles heading up. He braked and rolled down his window. "She's not there. Must have gone on foot."

One of the men shook his head. "We'll start a search."

Most likely they were looking for a body.

He rolled on down the road, swinging his head side to side, looking for signs of the woman.

If she was smart, she'd search for the cabin Raedke owned that sat lower on the mountain. That cabin perched slightly around the one side, more shielded from the weather, and could be reached on foot, by a determined person.

Was she determined enough?

He sure hoped so—he didn't relish finding her frozen to death in a snow bank.

The drive back down the mountain took longer under icy conditions. When he reached the bottom, he stared upward, squinting through the snow.

A gut feeling told him to look on the sheltered side of the mountain. He could go in on foot, but he'd ridden those trails in winter with a good horse and the right gear. Mentally, he compiled a list of essentials and drove back to the ranch quickly.

He'd no sooner reached it than Mimi was coming out of the house to meet him. "Dane's still not here," she said with concern on her face.

"He's a big boy. He'll find his way home." How many times had Zayden spoken those words about his father and now his brother too? "I'm going back up the mountain, and I'm taking the white horse. He's strong and got the balance for winter trails."

"You're searching for that woman, aren't you?" She gave a little shiver from standing in the cold or maybe from the idea of a woman lost outdoors.

"Yeah. I could use some things thrown into a pack if you don't mind—water, medicines, whatever you think she might need when I find her." He didn't say if he found her, because he didn't plan to fail.

In the barn, he gathered what he needed and began readying the horse for a ride. He hitched the horse trailer to his truck and guided the animal inside. Then he returned to the house and took the pack from Mimi. He gave her a perfunctory kiss on the cheek.

"Good luck, Zayden." She waved him away.

"I'll need it." He jumped behind the wheel and was off, driving to the base of the mountain where he could circle around and hit the trail less covered by snow.

It took him all of a few minutes to mount up and head for the trail. With the horse wearing a blanket but not one so thick that it would sweat and become chilled, and him in a heavy Carhartt, gloves and his cowboy hat pushed down over his ears, he settled in for a long journey.

The trail wasn't perfect, but he knew the lay of the land and took the best routes to spare the horse from a slip and conserve energy. A good amount of snow remained here, but the line of pines seemed to buffer some of the wind.

On the other side of the mountain, he caught the drone of snowmobile engines at times before the wind would howl again.

When was the last he'd been up here? Years, too many to count. If she knew of the cabin here in the lower elevation, she'd surely make her way to it. Was there even a cell tower that serviced this area? He doubted it.

With encouraging words to his mount, he guided them closer and closer to the cabin. As he neared the front door, he spotted a few footprints in the snow, and his heart grabbed in his chest.

Hastily, he moved the horse forward and jumped out of the saddle. After hitting the snow with a soft thump, he rushed to the door. Judging by the broken window pane, she'd been here. A fallen branch couldn't break out one pane of glass so perfectly.

He tried the doorknob and found it unlocked. He threw it wide and stepped into the cabin.

One glance revealed evidence she had been here at one point. But after a quick search, he only found warm ashes in the fireplace and… a scrap of black lingerie?

He gingerly picked the garment up so it dangled off a fingertip. "What the hell?"

* * * * *

I should have stayed at the cabin. At least it was warm and dry.

After wandering south on the mountain for what felt like hours, she didn't have a clue where she was. *Guess that makes me lost too.*

She definitely should not play the lottery this week—she was losing at every turn.

At least I'm not dead. The grim thought offered no boost of morale to get down the mountain faster. Getting off the trail sounded like a good idea, because the pines saved her from the icy blast of wind. But the pines didn't seem to be growing in the direction she wanted to go.

"Well, it worked once, right?" She eyed the pines and picked her way along the line, in search of some nice low-hanging branches.

Once she found a good place to sit and wait, she took a handful of snow in the palm of her glove and stuffed it into her mouth. It melted on her tongue, but did nothing to stave off her hunger or thirst. She ate another, ignoring the black conspicuous specks in the pristine white. Whoever said snow was clean had never eaten it.

She curled her knees up and dropped her head to them, fighting off tears of self-pity. She wouldn't waste the energy to cry, and she sure wouldn't shed a tear for Owen.

How many hours had she been out here now? The sun would soon be dipping over the horizon, and then she'd face a night alone in the elements.

A tear trickled down her cheek.

What felt like hours passed. A snuffing noise reached her, muffled but still an unusual sound. *Great – now I'll be eaten by wolves.*

The footsteps neared… then she heard a whinny.

On hands and knees, she scrambled out of her hiding place. Horse hooves appeared inches from her face, and a cry lodged in her throat.

She was about to call for help, but the rider wheeled the horse around and dismounted in one slick motion.

"Thank God," she cried.

He grabbed her by the shoulders, hazel eyes scanning her from head to foot. "What's your name?"

"Esme."

"How long have you been out here?"

"Too long."

"Can you stand? Never mind. C'mere." Without waiting for her reply, he scooped her into his arms. The warm strength of them enveloping her pulled more tears from her eyes. She allowed the weakness she'd been battling for hours to overcome her, trusting that this man would keep her safe.

"Can you put your arms around me? I'm going to lift you into the saddle."

Her frozen limbs complied when she ordered them to. He was broad, muscles flexing under her arms as he lifted her onto horseback as though she weighed nothing.

"Don't slip out of the saddle now. I'm going to mount behind you." No sooner had he spoken that, he settled behind her. She shuddered at the contact of his body, the heat melting her some.

"You're freezing. Here." A second later, a heavy woolen blanket landed over her front, and she was plastered to his warm body from behind. Her eyelids closed. Exhaustion overtook her.

"I got you, girl. Don't worry now."

She wouldn't—she was far too tired and would let her mystery rescuer do the worrying for both of them.

Chapter Three

The woman was more hair and big green eyes than anything. As Zayden drew her off the horse into his arms and carried her into the cabin, he couldn't help but think how long it'd been since he'd laid hands on the opposite sex.

She wore so many wet layers of clothing, he couldn't discern her size or shape, and right now, his first priority wasn't finding out. He had to get her warm and dry.

The sun steadily sank, and there was no way in hell he could get her down the mountain before darkness set in. Taking shelter in the cabin sounded like the best plan, and it had a small shed out back where he could keep the horse out of the elements.

First, the woman. Esme. What a strange name. But looking into her sea green eyes, he couldn't think of any name that would suit her better.

With her in his arms, he managed to open the cabin door and carry her to the sofa. She sat there, unmoving, and he wondered how far hypothermia had set in if she wasn't attempting to pull off her wet clothes.

He went for her gloves first. Soaked and heavy. He tossed them toward the fireplace and reached for the zipper of her coat. She stared at him while he removed the wet garment and tossed it aside too.

At least she wasn't only wearing a scrap of black lace and her boots were relatively dry.

He pulled these off next, followed by her socks, damp at the toes.

"You're lucky," he muttered. Wet feet usually meant a death sentence.

"I'm tired."

"I bet. First, we get you dry. Can you stand? I need to get you out of these wet pants."

Her eyes settled on his, the color like a gem at the bottom of a crystalline sea. "I can stand, but do I need to take off my pants?"

"Yes." His tone brooked no arguments. He took her by the upper arms and hauled her to her feet. She swayed a moment, but her hands worked to unfasten her jeans.

It took some awkward maneuvers to pull the wet denim off her feet, but he threw the jeans toward the fireplace too.

"Here. Wrap up in this." He tucked the blanket around her and moved to the fireplace. Kneeling before it, he stacked wood and kindling, crinkling some newspaper some nice camper had left behind. Seconds after lighting a match, the flames licked at the dry wood.

He grabbed the backs of two wooden kitchen chairs and dragged them to the fire, using one to drape the wet garments over, and returned to Esme.

Extending a hand, he studied her. "Come sit by the fire and warm up."

She nodded, not saying anything. He drew her to her feet, aware of how she only came up to the top of his chest. She still wore her hat, and he tugged it off as he set her in the chair.

Wild curls sprung out in all directions, honey brown and coiled tight from being wet. Something deep inside him gave a yank, like a rope on a cow's neck. But he ignored it and strode to the door.

"I've gotta see to the horse. Sit there and don't move, okay?"

"Can I get closer to the fire? It feels so good."

"I don't want you catching fire. That's close enough. I'll be right back."

Outside, he went to the shed. After a quick inspection, he determined it was large enough to shelter the horse but only if he emptied it of the contents. Which meant tossing cross-country skis and a couple old shovels out. Then he stripped the horse of its saddle and provided it one of the dry blankets from his pack, along with a bag of feed.

There was an old bucket in the shed he could use for water. He took this and went back inside the cabin. From a well someplace unseen, water flowed into the sink, rusty at first and then clearing. He filled the bucket and went back outside to the shed.

He realized he needed to send word to the others in the search party. He located his handheld radio and tuned to their channel. "This is Moon. I got her. We'll be staying in the cabin and coming down the mountain in the morning. She's all right, only suffering some exposure."

Before anyone could respond to his words, he switched off the radio. With the horse comfortable, he had to see to the woman.

She had scooted a bit closer to the fire, against his warning. He almost snorted at her breaking his rule and remembered how many times people had been pissed at him for disregarding theirs.

He fetched her some water and opened his pack to find a thermos of soup, long since cold, but he could heat it over the fire if he could find a pot.

The next few minutes were spent acting as camp cook, while Esme's green eyes followed his every movement. He found Mimi had stuffed a few cocoa packets in the backpack too, and he used water to make some in a mug.

Esme cupped this in her hands and released a long sigh. "It's so good to finally be warmer."

He touched the back of her hand where it was curled around the mug. It was still cold. "You could use a little more heat." He tossed another log on the fire and then stirred the soup. Outside, rain hit the windows and he remembered one pane was broken.

His gaze shot to the black lace tossed in the corner. "Were you here before?"

She nodded. "I remembered the cabin was here. I broke the window to reach in and unlock the door, but I couldn't stay long if I was going to get down the mountain before dark." She turned to look at the falling darkness. "We aren't going to make it either."

"No. We'll stay the night here and just focus on getting you warm, and then tomorrow we'll go down the mountain."

"Is your horse all right?"

"Yes. Tucked up in the shed with food and water."

She nodded, curls bobbing. "What's its name?"

He scratched his head. "I don't know."

"How can you not know your horse's name?"

"Ain't my horse." Except it was. Now.

She took this as the final word and sipped her cocoa. He spooned the hot soup into a bowl and balanced it on a metal plate he found in a cupboard to use as a tray. As she tucked in, eating with increasing enthusiasm with every spoonful, he eyed her.

Her boyfriend had abandoned her on the mountain—he might as well have left her for dead. But she wasn't bruised or battered, only windburned, a bit shocked…and beautiful.

"What happened?" he asked, low.

Her gaze flicked to his and then away. Her spoon scraped the bottom of the bowl, and she set it and the makeshift tray on the floor at her feet.

Awareness stole over him as he fought to keep from staring at her curves and thinking one slip of that quilt and he'd see bare skin glistening in the firelight.

He tried to look away and quit thinking about it, but soon he was glancing at her once more. Her face and throat glowed as she warmed… and it'd been a long time since Zayden felt a clutch of desire like this.

When a few minutes passed and she didn't speak, he said, "Well, he's clearly an idiot. Look at what he tossed away."

Her gaze locked on his for several heartbeats. "Thank you," she whispered.

She tugged the blanket tighter at the neck, but he saw the shake of her shoulders. Was it emotion taking hold or the hot soup warming her insides while the rest of her body needed to catch up?

He watched her a moment before he got up and held out his arms. "Come on. I'll put you in bed."

She nodded, shaking more visibly now, and he helped her to stand. Though the blanket slipped and he wanted to put his hands on all that glowing flesh, he secured the blanket again and guided her by the shoulder to the bed.

Being farther from the fire, the bedroom would offer less warmth, but there were plenty of warm blankets.

"Lie down." He pointed to the bed, and she awkwardly climbed in, her limbs no longer working well after being taxed for so many hours.

"I thought he was in the bedroom and when I came out, he was gone. I searched the cabin and that's when I saw he'd taken the truck and left me." Tears clogged her voice.

Zayden pulled the blankets over her curled form and watched her a moment as her teeth rattled.

There was no use for it—he had the body heat to warm the woman.

"Hell." He climbed into bed beside her and picked up the edge of the blanket. Her wide eyes burned into his. "May I share my heat with you? Sometimes it's the only way to warm up."

She hesitated, white teeth clamping on her plump lower lip. He nearly groaned—if seeing that was bad enough, how did he plan to cuddle those rounded curves, and with her wearing only a bra and panties?

Just as he thought she'd tell him to get away from her, she nodded. "I'm so cold. I thought that cocoa and soup would help, but I feel colder now." Her words came out in bursts of shivers.

He didn't waste any time and eased under the covers with her. When he slipped his arms around her, she didn't beat at him and cry rape, so he

47

continued to pull her into his embrace until she was nestled against his chest, with her legs snug against his.

"Put your feet between my calves. I can tell they're icy."

She nodded, and a big fluff of curls brushed his chin, catching in the stubble there. He didn't push them away, only kept her pressed to him.

Annnnnd now he wasn't only battling his good sense — he was about to pop a boner.

Her breasts were the full size of a man's palm, waist dipping to a flare of hips. Damn if he didn't want to grab them and part those round thighs. Or flip her over and explore that perfect ass.

She wasn't stick thin, and too bad, because then maybe he wouldn't be fighting off thoughts of gliding inside her and working her into a sweat. He liked his women with a bit of flesh to grab onto, and this one was tempting as hell.

But no, he wasn't an asshole, though there were plenty who'd argue that.

"Do you r-rescue women from the mountain all the t-time?" she asked through her quivering.

He planted a palm on her spine and drew her even closer. Her wild hair crept up around his mouth, and he pinned the curls down by resting his chin on the top of her head. If he talked, maybe he could take her mind off being cold — and her bastard of a boyfriend too.

"I grew up here and the mountain was an escape." Now why did he tell her that? He plowed on. "I know a lot about surviving in the elements."

"Did you take a class?"

"No. Once I ran away from home and spent a few nights up here. It wasn't February then, though, and the spring rains had already passed."

"How old were you?" She moved her hand as if trying to find a place for it to land. He caught it and placed it on his abs between them.

Maybe that's not such a good idea.

"I was eleven."

"Wh-what did you eat?"

"Trapped a rabbit and that lasted a day. After that, my luck ran out and I turned to searching for mushrooms and berries under the pines."

"I bet your parents were relieved when they found you."

He only grunted in reply.

How innocent, for her to believe his upbringing had been that of a normal American boy. When a couple firefighters making their usual run of the access roads on the mountain located him, they'd forced him home and probably been shocked to learn his father laid in a drunken stupor for two days and hadn't known he was missing. His kid brothers were plenty happy, though.

He held back a sigh and without thinking on it too much, let his hand wander over her spine, rubbing small circles.

"Owen and I spent the night in the cabin for Valentine's Day." Her words were quiet, restrained. "I really thought..."

He waited for her sugary voice, but she said no more.

"Did you have a fight?" he asked quietly.

She balled her fist on his abs and then shook her head. "I went into the bathroom to... never mind. But when I came out, he was just gone. No word, no note."

"How long have you been together?" He covered her fist with his hand and gently eased her fingers open. "Don't tense up. You need your blood flowing to get warm."

She sighed and relaxed. He didn't release her fingers where they remained trapped between them. He noted she no longer shivered, though he felt the cold seeping from her feet past the denim he wore.

"We've been dating for eight months. I thought... I'm stupid, I guess."

It dawned on him. It was Valentine's Day and her boyfriend brought her on a romantic mountain retreat, and she'd expected a much different outcome, probably ending with her wearing that lace number and sporting a fat diamond.

Damn, he hated knowing there were assholes out there who treated women this way. For all his problems in life, at least he was smart enough to realize he wasn't equipped for a relationship and steered clear.

He rubbed more circles on her spine, and she relaxed in his hold, head dropping forward so her cheek was pillowed on his chest.

People didn't usually trust him, not with the last name of Moon. But she didn't know him and was desperate to warm up.

She wiggled a little closer, all hips and breasts, and Christ, he shouldn't think about her.

How could he not, when she cuddled against him? He floundered for something to say.

"I'm sorry this happened to you, but I'm glad I found you."

She jerked her head suddenly, tipping it to look at him. "Are there others looking for me? Oh God, what a pain I am!"

"Not your fault. And I radioed the others in the search party — "

"Search party!"

" — and told them I found you. Don't worry about being trouble. The guys in Stokes have been out searching before and will again."

"But it was too stupid of me to be stranded."

"How was that your fault?" He raised his hand and brushed an errant curl from her eyes.

51

Pink flooded her cheeks, and she looked away again, but didn't attempt to leave his arms. In fact, she grew boneless, melting against him, and soon he knew sleep would overtake her and he'd be left lying here in torment, his dick a shaft of steel behind his zipper.

"You don't have any reason to feel guilty for having people out looking for you. The people who should feel guilty are idiots who aren't experienced hikers and go up the mountain without appropriate gear."

"Like you when you were eleven?"

He chuckled, the low rumble odd to his own ears. Didn't seem much to laugh about in life, especially right now. He suddenly wondered if Asher ever returned to the ranch, and if Mimi was now dealing with another younger drunk like his dad.

He'd been in Stokes all of a couple days and already he was taking responsibility for his brothers and worrying about them just as he had back in the day. They were old enough to handle themselves. So why did he feel the burn of anger with Asher or even Dane, who hadn't even bothered to show his face?

Suddenly, Esme rubbed her cheek against his chest and then fell still. He listened to her breathing, which had become deep and even.

She was asleep.

In his arms.

Soft and curvaceous—a living doll with beautiful green eyes and the most untamed hair he'd ever seen. Gently, he eased his head back so he could look down at her. When he saw the spikey lashes kissing her cheekbones, it was like a punch to the gut.

Quickly, he closed his eyes, willing his stupid protective inner workings to shut up. Just because he'd found her and she lay in his arms didn't make her his responsibility.

But hell if he didn't feel like going down the mountain tomorrow, hunting up this boyfriend of hers and busting his teeth out. The man *was* an idiot. Who would give this up, let alone jeopardize her?

He dragged in a full breath in an attempt to placate his anger and received a nose full of sweet woman.

Delectable woman.

Morning couldn't come soon enough.

* * * * *

Zayden. Esme let the name roll around in her mind. Maybe she was experiencing one of those crushes you get on your rescuer or a doctor who saved your life. But even so, the man was hot with a capital *H* and an extra *T*.

She'd woken to find herself alone in the bed, the blankets around her shoulders as if he'd tucked them there. After quickly dressing in her now dry clothes, she tentatively approached the cabin window. At

53

some point, Zayden had wedged some cardboard into the hole she'd made to break in.

It seemed like a lifetime ago that she'd been in such a terrible state of mind that she'd actually punched out the windowpane in order to reach inside the cabin and twist the lock. How low a person could become.

How low another person can make you.

She wasn't one of those girls who liked playing victim. In fact, anger boiled over, hotter than she'd experienced in her life, and that was saying something. She'd had more than one bum of a boyfriend, but she'd believed Owen was different. So far, he was the worst in the lot.

Through the window, she saw Zayden's big form as he saddled the horse in the snowy yard. Admiring his efficient movements, she slipped on her coat and walked outside.

He looked up and gave her a nod of greeting. "Warm enough now?"

She nodded. "Very warm. Thank you."

"No thanks needed. I'm glad I found you. I'll just finish here with the horse then come inside and gather our things. If you left anything that you'd like to pack..." He trailed off, not looking at her but at the saddle he fiddled with.

Her mind leaped straight to the black lace teddy she'd thrown out of her bag in a fit of rage the previous day. Thank God nobody had been around to witness that fit—or the crying jag that followed. She felt a bit stronger and owed it to Zayden.

Zayden's tone when he called Owen an idiot helped buoy her spirits. She was prepared to go down the mountain and face her life. First, she would thank those who helped in the search. Then she'd make sure her coworkers at the credit union knew she was okay. After that, she had quite a plan in store for Owen.

The son of a bitch.

"I'll pack up what's mine." She turned for the cabin door again. The fire continued to burn in the hearth, though only a few flames still lingered over the blackened logs. Who would come after them and inhabit this cabin? Lovers?

The door opened behind her, letting in an icy blast of wind, and then Zayden closed it. Across the room, their gazes met.

She should say something to him. "Thank you again, Zayden."

"I said no need." He strode to the table where his pack lay open. He rooted around in it and then held up a pair of heavy leather gloves. "My extra pair. You can wear them when we ride."

"Okay." A shyness stole over her. She knew his body well—the length, the breadth of his chest. How his heart thumped in a steady rhythm and how he smelled. They'd shared a night together, and didn't the saying go that a person could live a lifetime in one minute? She felt altered somehow.

It could be a matter of her faith being restored that not all men sucked big donkey balls. Sometimes strangers could take a stranger by the hand, and tell a girl she was safe and then share his body heat with her.

She shivered, and he locked his gaze on her. His rugged features had become familiar to her, and she could conjure the shape of his angled jaw and nose with a bump on the side from being broken, as well as his dark, hooded eyes. His hair skimmed his nape in soft whorls, projecting from under his cowboy hat.

"You're not gonna be warm enough, are you? Maybe you should stay here in the cabin and I'll ride down and get some extra winter things. A heavier parka, a—"

"I'm fine," she cut across him. "I'll be warm enough. Besides, we won't be lost out there the entire day, will we?"

"Don't plan on it." A smile ghosted over his lips, but only the corner of his mouth flickered upward. If she hadn't been staring at him, she would have missed it. He turned to his pack once more and began stowing away everything he'd brought with him.

She did the same, making a sweep of the cabin in case she'd left behind a sock. In the end, she stuffed the abandoned lace back in and zipped her bag shut. When they both had their bags in hand, he held out the gloves. She took them and slipped them on over her thinner neoprene ones.

He watched her close. "You're lucky to have all your fingertips today."

She nodded. "I never did find a spot of cell service on this entire mountain."

He grunted. "Next time you come up here, bring a satellite phone."

"Got it." She tapped her temple as if committing it to memory, and for her effort at a joke, Zayden rumbled a laugh.

He stood close, and she felt an urge to put her arms around him again, but refrained. She wasn't going to be a sappy, clingy woman. Besides, she'd spend the ride down the mountain in front of him in the saddle, his big chest at her back, and that would be plenty of physical contact.

Reaching up, she tugged her knit cap down over her ears, which only made her curls poof out the bottom more. Zayden's gaze traveled over her face and hair and then returned to her eyes.

"Let's go." He strode to the door, and she followed.

The horse pawed at the ground, raring to get on the move. Zayden said a few soft words to it, and she marveled at the trust between man and the beast he didn't even know the name of.

After getting settled in the saddle, he clicked his tongue, and they began to move.

She looked around herself, squinting at the blinding white of the snow against the sun, which had decided to come out. Of course, with her luck, the weather *would* take a huge turn. Why couldn't it have been nicer the previous day when she was on her own?

The snow drifted in places over the trail, but Zayden seemed to know where he was going and guided them with skill. Once they began to navigate a steeper incline, he scooted forward in the saddle.

"Lean forward. We've gotta keep the weight over the horse's shoulders and chest."

She did, and he locked an arm across her middle to hold her steady as they took the least evil route.

"What is the horse wearing on its feet? Snow boots?" she asked. She'd noticed the cute shoes before Zayden assisted her into the saddle.

"Hoof boots. They've got removable studs for traction. Was glad I found them in the barn."

"You live on a ranch?"

She felt him tense behind her, and the muscle of his arm hardened as well.

"I'm stayin' there for now."

She heard the cold tone of his voice and veered away from the topic.

"I work in the credit union in town."

"Yeah? Off Midland Street?"

"Yes. I'm a teller there, but I hope to move up someday."

"So banking is your passion."

She laughed, the sound caught by the wind. Zayden's arm relaxed, but he drew her a millimeter closer to his chest. She gladly accepted his protection as the wind picked up, blowing the horse's mane back.

"Not my passion, no, but it's a job I enjoy. Years ago, I started a degree in business and finance, but I didn't complete it."

"Wasn't for you anymore?" His voice washed past her ear.

"No, I quit school and followed a different jerk here to Stokes."

"You got a thing for jerks." It wasn't a question, and the statement rocked her deep. All she knew about herself was coming into focus, brought to light by a complete stranger.

Zayden didn't know her at all, but after thirty seconds of conversation he'd nailed her.

"Sorry. None of my business." He guided them across a flatter area, and the horse resumed its pace.

"You're good with horses."

"Grew up with them."

"I always wished I'd learned how to ride. We did a lot of outdoor sports in the Smoky Mountains when I was a kid back in Tennessee. That's why I was confident I could make it down the mountain."

"You probably would have been fine without that storm."

She nodded, and her hair caught on something — his coat zipper maybe. The soft tug of the strands released and another small shiver worked through her.

"So back to work tomorrow," he said.

"I guess."

"I can take you to the hospital to be checked out. Just in case," he added.

"I'm all right, but thank you anyway." The idea of saying goodbye to him gave her a hollow feeling in the pit of her stomach, like she'd just suffered a loss. Or Owen gave her that pang. She *was* out a boyfriend now, and she didn't even have a chance to tell him off. Now she had to see him again and find out why he'd done it.

A dozen scenarios moved through her mind while fighting to survive the storm. Had Owen really been about to propose and suffered cold feet? Or maybe she said something to send him packing? The worst thought by far was... did he really mean to abandon her on the mountain in a storm?

Stuff like that made TV movies on *Lifetime*, but was it really her boyfriend? His motive was sketchy, but she aimed to find out.

The ride down took a good two and a half hours, going at a slow pace. When they reached the road, she spotted an old truck and trailer parked there.

"That's mine," he said.

Her stomach churned with apprehension.

"You'll be happy to get home."

She didn't respond.

"Esme?"

God, he said her name in a low rumble that spread through her entire system.

She shook herself. "I'm not that excited about answering any questions that will come."

"You got family here?"

"No. They're in Tennessee. But my coworkers will want to hear the story. I'm just hoping there isn't a newspaper reporter waiting for me when I return."

"I don't know about that. Stokes didn't have a newspaper when I left." He flexed his arm around her middle, and the small movement sent a jerk to her heart.

"You haven't lived here all the time?"

"Nah. Got out."

Since he didn't expand on this statement, she remained silent as they approached the truck. He reined in the horse and dismounted, then reached up for her.

Wordlessly, she slipped into his arms. Was it her imagination, or did he hold onto her a beat longer than necessary? She steadied herself, watching him move to the trailer and open the door. He led the horse inside and waved to her.

"Get in the truck and out of the wind."

She did. In a strange man's truck, she looked around. It was empty of all but a few coins in the cup holder. Either he'd just cleaned it out or he wasn't a guy who personalized his vehicle. Every man she knew had a gun rack or stickers for a shooting group, Mountain Dew bottles, and Cheetos bags on the floor.

Zayden's truck looked as if it belonged to no one.

She twisted to look out the rear window but couldn't see him behind the trailer. So she faced forward and watched in the side mirror as he appeared. Seconds later, he climbed behind the wheel.

He gave her a glance before starting the engine. "Where am I dropping you?"

"At my apartment. I live in a rental in the old part of town."

"All right. Holler when we get close."

"Okay." She released a heavy sigh.

Silence descended, and her thoughts bounced from Owen to her ordeal and skidded sideways to how she'd have to discuss everything at work.

"The house is just there. The blue one."

He drew up in front of the place and looked at her. "You sure you don't need to go to the hospital?"

She shook her head. "I just need a hot shower and my bed."

Without another word, he climbed out of the truck and moved to her side before she could step out. He assisted her to the ground, a hand on her arm even though she didn't need it.

"I didn't even say thank you to your horse."

A flicker of amusement crossed his handsome face. "He'll understand."

Looking into his eyes, she smiled. "You were great up there."

"I did what any decent man would."

"That isn't true. And I don't only mean getting me safe and warm. You said some things that made me feel better."

His brow crinkled, and she noticed a slice through it from a scar. "What's that?"

"You made me feel like I might not be such a loser."

His brows shot up, and he gave her that look again—like he wanted to move in closer and put his hands on her in a very sexual way.

"You're far from a loser, Esme."

She nodded. "You reminded me I have worth."

"Don't let that bastard make you feel like a castoff. Ya hear?" The vehemence in his tone took her aback. She blinked and then reached up to put her arms around his neck, sneaking a touch of his hair to see if it was as soft as it looked. Actually, it felt softer, like goose down.

He squeezed her back briefly and then stepped away. "Maybe I'll see ya around. Take care of yourself."

She nodded. He paused, looking down at her. For a heart-pounding moment, she wondered if he might kiss her, and if she wanted him to. What did that make her, when twenty-four hours before, she'd been hoping for a ring from another man?

She must have suffered some frostbite to the brain up there on that mountain.

He watched her with that hooded stare that was doing questionable things to her insides. Then he said the most perfect thing.

"If ya need me to break his legs for ya, gimme a call."

Chapter Four

Zayden reached the gates of the ranch and rolled to a stop to look up at the wooden sign with metal letters spelling out *MOON RANCH*. Any passerby would see that sign and think the ranch was something special and not the source of years of pain to him and his brothers.

But it could be something, now that the old man's dead.

His mind shot back to his talk with Mimi and how the Ute said you shouldn't waste good land.

The problem never lay in the property all those years but rather in the management of it. Looking back, he had to shake his head in wonder at how they'd managed to keep the place at all. At thirteen, he'd taken over much of the running of it, and by sixteen had fully stepped into those boots.

In his youth, he saved the ranch. Could he again?

Did he want to stick around to see?

As he released the brake and rolled down the driveway, he mulled this over, but it wasn't a question to be answered in a few minutes' time. He had a lot to consider.

After seeing to the horse, he walked to the house. Silence reigned inside, and he found a note on the kitchen counter from Mimi, saying she'd gone into town for supplies with her great-nephew. Asher appeared nowhere to be found, and by this point, Zayden didn't expect for Dane to turn up.

A sudden bone-deep weariness hit him. He'd barely slept a wink with that soft woman in his arms all night, and he was dragging. Scrubbing a hand over his face, he walked into his old bedroom and kicked off his boots. The space looked tidy, with stacks of old horse trader magazines tucked under the battered dresser. Some of them he'd stolen from the Stokes library. Sometime in his absence, Mimi had replaced the curtains, and the pale blue cloth partially covered the big window overlooking the back field.

His comforts forgotten, he wandered to the window and looked out. The land resembled a photograph, meandering right up to the base of the mountains. Even if the Moons didn't own all that, they had the view.

The shades of slate blue and white of the mountains reminded him of his recent adventure...and then a set of sea-green eyes loomed in his mind's eye.

With a grunt, he turned away from the view and walked into the one bathroom the entire household shared. Mimi cleaned it as well, and the fresh towels stacked on a shelf invited him to strip off his clothes and turn the shower on as hot as it could go.

When he stepped under the spray, he closed his eyes. His time with Esme lingered in the back of his mind, along with the more pressing confusion of what lay before him.

Stay or go? The question of the damn day.

He quickly scrubbed away the grime of two days on the mountain and pictured Esme in a hot bath, golden limbs beaded with water droplets and her curls springing around her face...and her damp curls between her thighs.

He slammed a mental door on that thought and stepped out of the shower onto the bathmat. After a brisk rub of the towel, he wrapped it around his waist and walked out of the bathroom in a fog of steam.

He stopped dead. "You look like shit."

Asher reeked of booze and cheap perfume. Could it get any more cliché than that? Yeah, it could — like father like son.

"Not all of us can be fresh as a rose like you, Z." Asher leaned heavily against the wall. By Zayden's guess, he couldn't stand upright for long.

"Go sleep it off, Ash. Then get a shower. I could use some help around the place."

Asher grinned. "Takin' over like old times?"

"Don't know yet, but there's things to be done, and leaving it all on Mimi ain't fair." He walked past Asher and through his open bedroom door. He slammed it behind him and heard a gratifying, "Goddammit," from Asher, who was most likely nursing one hell of a headache.

Serves him right. Dumb ass.

Minutes later, tanked up with coffee and one of Mimi's cinnamon rolls, he strode to the barn. If Mimi's great-nephew came today, it was only to take his great-aunt to town and not do chores. With a lot to do for the horses, Zayden settled in with a pitchfork and a wheelbarrow.

The work felt good, but he couldn't say for sure about being back on the ranch. Did he want this for himself? For the past decade he'd rarely considered what he wanted, just drifted through life. During one of his father's lucid spells where he resolved to get off the drink, he gave Zayden some advice. Make his mark and go with his gut. He'd said a lot of other things that he'd forgotten, but those two bits stuck with him.

His gut led him astray at times, like when he'd beat up that guy on the construction team for being careless and nearly getting several of them killed, him included. After sitting in jail for a week and paying some hefty fines, on top of losing his job, he realized dear old daddy, even in his sober moments, wasn't much good to him.

On the flip side, he'd gone with his gut instinct to circle the mountain and had found Esme. When something good came out of his actions, it pushed him to put more faith in his gut.

What was it saying right now?

The cold air in his lungs was tinged with the scents of horse and hay, and he welcomed it. When he got one stall cleared out, he sprinkled fresh bedding inside and moved to the farthest stall where a mare stood dozing.

He opened the wooden door and reached out to stroke the horse's nose. Right away, he saw she wasn't okay.

"C'mon, girl." He urged her out of the stall so he could look her over better.

She came hesitantly, sluggishly. When she extended her neck downward, he suspected what was up. Quickly, he checked her nostrils and sure enough, discharge seeped out.

"Shit. You got choke." He'd seen veterinarians address the problem, but he wasn't confident he could on his own.

After examining her a bit more, the mare made a coughing noise, and that solidified his diagnosis.

"Dammit." He led the horse out into the paddock and strode back to the house. An old-fashioned phone clung to the wall with a list of numbers taped beside it. The vet clinic was halfway down, and he dialed the number.

When the receptionist heard his name, she paused. "Moon?"

"Yeah. Out Evergreen Road."

"I know where you are. It's just that, you're on our no-response list."

"What the hell is a no-response list?"

"It means at some point too many bills went unpaid, and we've cut you off from further services."

Dammit. He stared at the wall. Leave it to his father to fuck him over even in death.

"I can pay," he said.

"Hold please."

The wall in front of him had been patched more than once, after his father drove his fist through the plaster. Zayden himself had mixed the plaster and smeared it over the holes, over and over. His inexperienced attempts now were glaringly ugly, but Mimi painted over them without a word back then.

Just like everything in this goddamn place— problems were slapped with a coat of paint and ignored.

No more.

"What is the problem you need to see Dr. Cody for?" the receptionist asked, jarring him from his dark thoughts.

Dr. Cody was a new name to him, but it didn't matter. "One of the horses is choked."

"How long have the symptoms been going on?"

"I don't know. She seemed fine to me yesterday, so recent. Look, is Dr. Cody coming out or not? Because I don't have time to give you financial proof that I can pay the bill, but I will."

"She'll be out to the ranch within the hour."

"Good. Thank you," he added before hanging up.

Great—what sort of bill was he looking at? He suddenly remembered the nice fine balled up on the floor of his truck. He'd been in Stokes all of a few days and was already in over his head. He didn't currently have a bank account, and all the cash he had in the world was in his back pocket.

He had no choice, though. The livestock came first on a ranch, always, even if he didn't want the responsibility.

Back in the paddock, the horse hadn't moved, just hung its head and coughed. He got together what he thought the vet would need—a bucket of water and one of the thin plastic hoses used to put through the horse's nose and down its throat so they could flush whatever was stuck in its esophagus.

When he heard the crunch of tires on gravel, he walked out to see who'd arrived. The unfamiliar truck could belong to Mimi's great-nephew, but a woman wearing jeans and a barn coat got out, so he went to greet the vet.

"Dr. Cody?" he asked with a cock of his brow.

She gave him a once-over. "You must be one of the Moon brothers."

"Zayden. I'm the oldest."

"Sorry to hear about your father." Her brown hair was pulled into a ponytail on her nape, and the strands fluttered in the breeze.

"I'm not," he said for the third time since hearing about his dad.

She looked up at him. Amusement flashed in her eyes and instantly disappeared. "Show me to the horse."

He did. She diagnosed the mare with choke and within minutes was flushing warm water through her in an attempt to free the blockage, while he lent a hand as directed.

"There it goes. The water's moving freely now. Okay, keep her quiet for a day. Give her some hay to graze but don't let her overeat. We need her gut to recover after not working for a while."

He gave a nod. "Thank you for coming out, Doctor. I appreciate it."

She sent him a long look. "You realize this ranch owes me a substantial sum."

"How much?"

"Thirty-two hundred."

Jesus.

"That much?" He kicked at a clump of grass in the paddock. What could they sell to get that amount?

"That much," she repeated. Her expression told him she expected not only to be paid for today's visit, but what they owed for past ones as well.

He noted movement in the yard and spotted Asher coming toward them. Circling the topic of vet bills, Zayden waved to his brother. "This is my brother, Asher."

"Hello." She turned to him but only briefly. "About that bill."

"Yeah, about that." Zayden rubbed a hand over his nape. "I don't have all of it right now."

Her brows shot up.

"But I can get it. Maybe not all at once, but you'll be paid, I promise." When she shot him a skeptical look, he said, "Not all Moons are trash. I keep my word. Look, you did a fantastic job here today, and I'm sure in the past for our father too. You deserve to be paid for your services, and I'm sorry this has gone unpaid so long."

Leaning against the fence, Asher ducked his head to hide a smile.

"Look at this horse. She seems to be feeling so much better already."

Dr. Cody reached out to stroke the mare's neck. "I'm glad she's better, and I'm only doing my job."

"Will you accept payments if I put it into writing that you'll get your money?" Zayden offered her a smile.

She delivered one more pat to the mare's neck and bent to pick up her bag of supplies. "Your word's enough, Moon. Just don't make me sic the sheriff on you for failure to pay. Got it?"

"Thank you, Doctor. I'll see you to your truck and give you the first installment in cash." He did what he promised and when he returned to the paddock, Asher was still standing there, grinning his cheesy grin.

"The fuck are you smiling about?" Zayden asked.

"Z, you still got it, don't you? That Moon charm."

He huffed out a breath in response and started back inside the barn to finish the chores he'd begun hours ago.

Asher followed. "Remember Dad would run out of cash and his tab at the bar was full, but he'd still talk people into buying him another drink. You got it too. You sweet-talked that vet into taking payments from an account she's had frozen for years."

"Didn't have much choice. We need every animal we got on this ranch earning us money." He hoped to hell he didn't use whatever skills he had for the wrong reasons.

Asher chuckled. "I'm still in awe of your skills, big brother."

"Stop being in awe and make yourself useful." He tossed him a manure fork, which he caught onehandedly. Together, they worked in companionable silence a while.

"What do you think one o' these horses is worth?" Zayden jerked his head toward the field, where half a dozen good horses grazed.

Asher followed his movement. "Dunno. That white one would fetch the best price."

"I can't understand how Dad even held on to these animals. Where was the money coming from?"

His brother shrugged. "Where did it ever come from? We Moons are resourceful. You'll figure out how to get this place running again."

Pausing in his work, he turned to look at Asher. "What makes you think I'm stayin' on?"

"You have a connection to this place."

"You don't?" Zayden tossed more dirty shavings into the wheelbarrow to cart out.

"Not the same as you. I've always been along for the ride, but you were the one steering the ship." Asher propped his fork in a corner and grabbed the handles of the wheelbarrow. "I'll dump this."

Zayden watched him go, his mind rioting with all he knew of the ranch, his family, and himself. The ranch and family he understood. His real question lay with himself. The man he'd become over the past ten years wouldn't for a moment consider staying here, but here he was thinking of selling a horse to get quick cash for the place.

Looking out the barn door, he saw the white gelding trotting across the field. Asher was right—it would be worth most. But Zayden thought he'd sell one of the others first.

* * * * *

Esme smiled at the customer in front of her. "Welcome to People's Credit Union. What can I do for you today?"

The woman studied her. "You're the woman who was lost on the mountain a couple of days ago, aren't you?"

Feeling her cheeks burn, she said, "Yes, but I'm here now. Are you cashing a check?"

"What happened anyway? Your boyfriend dump you?" The nosy woman wasn't the first customer to come into the credit union and drill her about her ordeal, and she was getting sick of the attention. As if she didn't feel stupid enough for having chosen Owen as a boyfriend, the whole town of Stokes seemed bent on driving it home.

She offered the woman a smile in hopes that she'd begin to feel some of the calm she portrayed on the outside. "Cashing a check?" she prompted again.

Seeing that Esme wasn't willing to answer her question, the woman slid a check across the counter. Esme took it and began processing it. "Would you like this deposited?"

The transaction took a few minutes, and thankfully the woman left without more questions. The next in line stepped up, and Esme gave the gentleman the same smile.

"How can I help you, sir?"

"Wanted to see for myself if you had lost a finger or two to frostbite, but seems like you got all ten." The man's drawled words struck her with irritation.

"Yep, got both working hands. Thanks for asking."

"Heard you wandered that mountain for a full day."

God, didn't anybody have anything else to talk about? Surely there was some other news to occupy these people's time.

"What can I do for you today?" She ignored his interest in her life, and he soon left as well. By the time her break came, she couldn't wait to sneak off to the breakroom and be alone.

She'd barely uncapped her iced tea when her coworker, Natalie, came in.

"See you got all your fingers," she said as she breezed by her to the mini fridge and took out her lunch.

Esme groaned and plastered a hand over her face. "I'm so tired of talking about it. The people of Stokes need a life."

"You're just now figuring that out, girl?" She smiled at Esme and popped her plastic container into the microwave. While it warmed, Natalie looked her over. Concern pulled her brows together. "You sure you're okay?"

"Positive."

"Owen seems like such a good guy. He must have had a good reason for leaving," Natalie said.

Esme's brows shot up. "If he did, he didn't tell me. That might have been helpful before he just stranded me without transportation or the ability to call for help." Anger washed through her—she was sick and tired of men who acted badly and their indiscretions were pushed off as minor. She liked Natalie, but she wasn't going to brush off Owen's actions on the mountain because he seemed like a "good guy."

Her friend chewed her lower lip, and Esme waved a hand at her. "Out with it. Just ask whatever it is you want to ask, because I've probably already heard it today."

"I wondered if you'd heard from Owen."

Her stomach pitched between anger to despair at the mention of her boyfriend yet again. No, her ex. Definitely her ex—the man didn't even deserve a glance from her after what he'd done.

She did feel she could trust Natalie with the story. "I haven't heard a word from him."

"You didn't try to call?"

She gave a hard shake of her head and drank some tea while Natalie fetched her meal from the microwave and sat down at the break table with it.

She looked over Esme. "You're not eating?"

"I had a big breakfast this morning," she lied. Fact was that her appetite had fled since her time on the mountain.

"All right," she said with a suspicious ring to her voice and dug into her chicken and vegetables.

Esme watched her for a moment, her own stomach knotted. What was she going to do about Owen? She deserved some answers, and it was clear he wasn't going to provide any unless she demanded them. The idea of picking up the phone and calling or texting him made her stomach hurt, though.

"Here, have some of my grapes. I can't eat them all." Natalie pushed another container across the table, and Esme sank to one of the chairs and took a grape.

The sweetness lay on her tongue, but didn't whet her appetite any more. In fact, she felt a little nauseated. After only two grapes, she pushed the container back.

"Thank you."

Natalie gave her a soft smile. "I know you're new to Stokes, that you came here to be with a man. That didn't work out and now Owen..."

"I don't want to discuss it," she said quietly.

"I'm just trying to say that you can talk to me. And if not me then somebody else."

She arched a brow at her friend. "Jason?"

Natalie's gaze met hers, and they both burst out laughing at the mention of their stiff bank manager who had actually asked Esme about her scenic trip.

"If you talked to our manager more than one time a day, Esme, the man would follow you around like a puppy." After that shocking statement, Natalie took a bite and chewed.

"What on earth are you talking about?"

"He looks at you all the time."

"I don't notice it. He doesn't look at me any more than he looks at anyone else who works here."

Natalie offered her an expression that said differently.

Esme shivered. "Ew. Just ew. Anyway, the last thing I need is more interest from a guy. I've got my hands full with dumping Owen."

"Wait—you haven't dumped him yet? Or did he really dump you by leaving?"

Somehow, Natalie's words didn't irritate the way anyone else's would if they'd asked her the same question.

She shook her head. "I'll figure it out. I'm going to relax and finish my tea before I have to deal with more people asking if I'm really missing a big toe. Where the hell do these rumors come from?"

Natalie giggled. "You should limp around a little, let them think it's true."

She groaned. "That's the last thing I need."

"I do have one question for you and then I won't ask any more." Natalie centered her focus on her.

"What is it?"

"The man who rescued you. Is it really Zayden Moon?" She pitched her voice lower.

Esme tipped her head. "It was Zayden. Why? Do you know him?"

"I know of him. He and his family have been the talk of Stokes for many years. His youngest brother Asher graduated with my oldest sister, the one who lives up in Juniper Bush now with her husband and three kids?"

She nodded, though she didn't know a thing about her sister.

Natalie leaned over the table. "Their father just died a few days ago, and the brothers are all back in town."

"For his funeral." Esme's stomach swam with even more regret than it had been since her day on the mountain. She'd ripped a man away from grieving for his father to come and search for her on the mountain. She bit off a groan.

"I'd say that's why Zayden's in town."

"When is the funeral?"

"Should be today or tomorrow."

"Will it be announced in the newspaper?" He'd told her Stokes didn't have a paper when he'd left — now it did. Luckily, the article about her being lost was small and hadn't made the headline.

"Maybe, but you aren't planning to go, are you?" Natalie popped a grape in her mouth.

She could never show up at the church or cemetery, so it didn't matter. She wouldn't intrude on Zayden's grief, but was truly sorry her stupidity gave Zayden more worry in this already stressful time.

She placed the cap on her tea and put it back into the fridge. "I'm going out to face the next influx of gossip."

Natalie smiled. "Make sure you limp."

Esme faked dragging her foot until she reached the breakroom door and then walked normally to the sound of Natalie's laughter following her.

She threw a glance toward Jason's office as she resumed her position on the line and found him looking at her. He glanced down at his paperwork, but it left an icky feeling of dread that Natalie could be right about his interest.

It didn't matter, because she wasn't interested in any man, let alone a forbidden office affair. She was through with guys — burnt twice.

Her mind shot back to Zayden Moon. On the mountain, she must have been so preoccupied with herself that she hadn't noticed a single hint of sadness on the man's rugged features. How horrible of her. If she ever got the chance to apologize to him, she would, but if he left Stokes after the funeral, Esme may not ever see him again.

* * * * *

Cold-calling the neighbors and asking if they'd be interested in buying a horse was on Zayden's to-do list today, along with taking off the damn tie trying to choke him to death.

When he tore it off his neck, Asher laughed. "Don't know why you bothered dressing up for that motherfucker's funeral. Told ya the old man wouldn't care if you showed up in your underpants."

"I don't know why I wore it either," he muttered and loosened the top three buttons of a dress shirt he'd located in the far rear of his closet. He'd drawn the line at suit pants, though — his jeans and boots had done just fine for the short service and five minutes it had taken to dump his father's casket into a hole in the ground.

Zayden might have dressed for the occasion, but it was Asher, always Asher, who'd shown enough

82

respect to toss a handful of dirt over the casket. Zayden had turned and walked away. And Dane hadn't shown up at all.

As Mimi entered the living room bearing a tray of sandwiches and tea, Asher looked up with a smile. Zayden started to thank her and realized he had more to say.

"I'm thinkin' of stayin' on here at the ranch."

Her blue eyes sparkled. "Thought you might, son."

Not for the first time, he realized Mimi was more his family than the asshole who shared DNA with them. But she was just as screwed up as he and his brothers were. To the bitter end, she'd enabled Chaz Moon's behavior by continuing to cook and clean for him. They were all to blame.

She swayed her gaze to Asher. "What about you, Ash? You plan to make a home here again?"

He heaved himself to his feet. "Actually, no. I'll be heading out this afternoon."

Zayden's chest tightened. When he lost his brothers to the far scatters of the country, it continued to haunt his daily life. Over the years, he'd blamed himself for being out of touch with family, and then he'd come to terms with the fact that just because you shared a bad upbringing didn't mean you had to be friends into adulthood.

Still, it stung.

He reached out a hand, and Asher took it. The hard clasp of their hands felt like a bond to Zayden, and for now, it was enough.

"Good luck in whatever you do."

"Thanks, Z."

"If you run across our brother out in the world, kick his ass for me."

"Will do." Asher's crooked grin reminded him of many more adventures of kids. It hadn't all been bad, and what was good, they made for themselves.

Zayden pulled him into a hug, and they thumped each other's backs while Mimi dabbed her eyes with a tissue she produced from up her sleeve. When they drew apart, Zayden cleared his throat.

"I'm heading over to Schumer's to see if he may be interested in buyin' one of the horses."

"Knowin' you and that Moon charm, you'll come away with more than it's worth." Asher looked to Mimi, who openly cried now. "Awww, c'mere, darlin'. Give me a hug." He enfolded the dear woman against his chest and shot Zayden a look that said *take care of her.*

Zayden nodded. *Guess if I'm takin' responsibility, I'm going all the way.*

Chapter Five

Esme came out of the money vault and shut the heavy metal door behind her. With a bundle of one-dollar bills in hand, she moved toward her station and began filling her money drawer.

"Wow." The feminine sigh from behind made her look up just as a tall hunk of a man crossed the credit union lobby. A man who was all too familiar to Esme, since she'd spent a night cuddled against his chiseled body.

Natalie and another teller named Allison huddled together, whispers flying.

Esme followed Zayden's progress across the room. Jason stepped out of his office. He caught Esme staring and glanced at Zayden.

Quickly, Jason intercepted him. "Can I help you?"

"Here to talk to the loan officer." Zayden's deep voice cut a wide swath through the female workers. While Natalie and Allison stopped whispering, Esme's pulse quickened.

"Do you have an appointment?" Jason asked him.

Zayden's posture spoke a thousand volumes. The hard set of his shoulders and how he braced his boots on the tile floor said he wasn't a man who made appointments.

"All right, then. Step into my office please." Jason waved him inside.

As Zayden vanished through the door and it closed behind him, Esme dragged in a deep breath.

"Oh. My. God. He is hotter than I imagined a bad boy like one of the Moons to be." Allison's statement made Esme twist to look at her and Natalie.

"I can't believe that's the man who rescued you, Esme!" Natalie's quiet squeal had her glancing around. Thankfully, no customers were in the building at this moment, besides the topic of discussion, who was enclosed in Jason's office.

He was here for a loan, and his father had been buried the previous week. Did that mean he planned to stay in Stokes?

She found herself ignoring the questions thrown at her by her coworkers and stared at her boss's door. When Roberta, one of the older ladies who also handled loans, left her desk in the corner to bustle over and join the discussion, Esme wished she could sink in to the floor.

"You spent the night with *him*?" the older woman asked.

"Yes, but it was very respectable," she shot back.

"Honey, you are holding out on us." Natalie wagged a finger at her.

"There's nothing to tell!" More flustered than she should be, she bit down on her lower lip and stole another look at the closed door.

"Those Moons are no good, but they're gorgeous." This from Allison.

She whirled to pierce the woman in her stare. "Why are they no good?"

"Their daddy was the town drunk. Held down a barstool more than he was ever at home raising those boys."

Esme's heart gave a small squeeze of sympathy for Zayden and the brothers she knew little of.

"I heard from Deputy Shawn Dickinson that he pulled Zayden Moon over as soon as he rolled into town and he…" she pitched her voice low, "has a record."

Esme blinked. "For what?" she heard herself ask.

"If it's too bad, he won't be given a loan. We're about to find out."

What could Zayden have done to get a criminal record? A host of crimes rumbled through her mind, but she couldn't picture the man who'd rescued her committing armed robbery or murdering anyone.

The ladies were discussing this now in hushed tones.

She shook her head and broke into the conversation. "He wouldn't do those things."

"How do you know?" Natalie asked.

"Because he's not that sort of person." At most, Zayden would get into a bar fight.

"Maybe it was a fight," Natalie said as she thought it. "Would he get into a fight? A man with muscles like that could do some real damage."

"He did offer to break Owen's legs if I want him to," she said to herself. But the ladies latched right onto that, and soon she was thwarting the threat before it became a rumor.

Relief filled her when a couple customers entered, and they were all occupied for the time being. She continued to toss inconspicuous glances toward her boss's door. Long minutes passed, and just when she was beginning to wonder if Zayden might have leaped out the window instead of using the door like everyone else, the door opened.

Both tellers whipped around to look, and Esme struggled to appear more nonchalant.

"Oh. My. God."

Here they go again, she thought of her flippant coworkers. But as soon as Zayden lifted his head and met her gaze, a spike of attraction hit her.

Breathing faster, she tried for a smile and threw him a wave.

When he sauntered forward, he might as well be a celebrity for all the attention he was garnering. And in worn jeans, scuffed boots, that sexy-as-sin hat, a plain black T-shirt and a flannel, no wonder. *Walking sin.*

"Shhh!" one of the girls said from behind her, but Esme ignored everyone as Zayden approached.

He paused in front of her station and gave her a crooked smile. "How you feelin'?"

Either Natalie or Allison swallowed a giggle. Hell, at this point, it could be Roberta.

Esme struggled for composure. Looking up at Zayden now, she wondered how she had the guts to curl up against him, let alone sleep in his arms. That night remained a haze of fear and pain, and she had nothing to be embarrassed about, but that didn't stop the flush from creeping up her throat.

"I'm fine now, thank you," she managed.

"Glad to hear it," he drawled out, his gaze darting upward to her hair. Today she'd wrangled all her curls into a big barrette on the back of her head but the wayward strands had a horrible habit of escaping. God, she hoped she didn't look like Bozo the Clown right now.

Reaching up, she smoothed a hand over her head, but didn't feel anything coming loose.

"Good to see you in here," she said stupidly. If she could bite off her own tongue or tramp on her own foot, she'd do it.

"Just talkin' to the manager." His brows tipped down in the center, but the scowl made him sexier.

More rustling noises came from behind her, and she glanced back to see Natalie holding a sheaf of papers over her face as she spoke to Allison.

She spun forward again. Zayden also took notice of what was happening behind her. He didn't appear to be surprised—he probably saw this behavior every time he walked out of the house.

"Well, I'd best be going. I've got more errands to run." He looked right into Esme's eyes and smiled, and her heart took off pattering even faster.

He made it as far as the door before she called out to the others, "I'm taking my break!" and ran for the exit.

She caught up to Zayden on the sidewalk out front. "Zayden, wait a moment!"

He stopped and studied her with that slow perusal that reminded her of their time on the mountain, squashed together into the saddle...and in bed.

"I...um...wanted to thank you again."

"Sweetheart, no need. I said so before." He latched his gaze onto her lips and then slowly dropped it over the length of her body, leaving her feeling like a hot dog on a skewer held to the campfire. She burned with instant awareness of this impossible connection they'd somehow forged that day.

"All right," she said, lifting a hand to her hair as she often did when nerves kicked in. "Well, I wondered if I might get your phone number."

The corner of his lips tipped up, and she went weak in the knees. Thank God the other girls weren't out here to see it. She wouldn't put it past Allison to fall flat on her face and make a scene.

"Why? You need rescued again?" His words washed over her like a lover's caress. Soft words she could barely focus on the meaning of, because the sound of them reminded her of pure seduction.

"I might." Hers came out breathless.

"You got your phone on you?"

She didn't. What an idiot.

"I'm not allowed to have my phone while I'm working. Um…just recite your number to me and I'll remember it."

He arched a brow as if he didn't buy her line. The ten digits he spoke shouldn't sound dirty to her ears, but they did. Somehow, she managed to commit them all to memory and in the right order—at least she hoped so.

"Thanks. Well, I'll see you around maybe. Good luck with your loan, Zayden."

He gave a nod and without another word, continued down the sidewalk and crossed the lot to his old truck.

She stood rooted in place a moment, watching him, admiring his long strides and the way his ass filled out those jeans so well.

A shiver ran through her, reminding her she was outside without a coat, and it was February.

Since she was still on her break, she figured it was time to stop being a weenie and actually call out

Owen for what he'd done and went back inside. At least nobody sat in the breakroom pummeling her with questions about Zayden when she made the phone call. Owen picked up on the third ring with a sheepish tone to his voice.

"Esme."

"Owen, I—"

"Look, I'm so sorry, Esme. I was a huge idiot that day, and I've thought about what I did a lot over the past few days. I never should have done it. I panicked and I want to make it up to you."

Fat chance of that, when her heart was already in another country as far as he was concerned. However, she did want to hear his side just to have closure on the entire ordeal.

"Let me take you out tonight. You deserve to be treated to something fancy. That new steakhouse is open, and it's a packed house every night from what I hear, but one of my buddies knows the owner, and I can get us in."

There it was—the Owen she knew. She wouldn't fall for his sweet-talk anymore. But going out with him meant she would hear his reasons for abandoning her on a mountain during a storm. What was the worst that could happen? She'd go to a swanky steakhouse with her ex and end up paying for her own dinner?

"Seven o'clock." Her tone was no-nonsense.

"I'll pick you up at your place."

"No. I'll meet you there, Owen."

He sighed into her ear. "I really am sorry, Esme. I screwed things up."

A weight bore down on her. Things had been good between them at one time. Up until the moment she realized he'd left her at the cabin without transportation, she hadn't suspected anything was amiss.

No, this was not a date. They were not getting back together. She only needed closure. She didn't want him back, no more than she wanted that bum she'd followed to Stokes back. She was a strong woman who could stand on her own — she didn't need a man.

She ended the call, already planning the killer dress and heels she'd wear to prove her ex had made one heck of a bad decision in dumping her. She also had a deadly speech written in her mind, and she would tell him off in front of the whole restaurant.

Or…maybe she'd put in that call to Zayden and have him come down and break his legs.

* * * * *

Zayden looked around the barn. Making this ranch turn a profit would be a longshot. But if he did have a dose of the Moon charm, then he hoped it worked on that manager at the credit union.

The guy didn't seem very impressed with Zayden's plans to expand by purchasing fifty head of cattle to start or provide a small wage to Mimi's great-nephew for working there, but both those things were valid when it came to ranchin'.

He wandered across the yard to the house and sank to the porch step. The land snoozed. It was too early for night animals, but as a kid he always loved sitting in this very spot and trying to spot the critters. Those times he'd spend dreaming of getting the hell out of Stokes and far away from his father.

With his father buried up the road and the ranch passing into his hands as soon as the paperwork finished filing, he considered how his dreams had changed.

Would he be able to find any peace in this work? He'd failed to locate that elusive dream even after he escaped and struck out on his own, but he didn't have anything to lose either.

The cold from the wood seeped into his backside, and a gust of wind sent snowflakes dancing faster in the air, but he dragged icy breaths into his lungs and relished the taste on his tongue.

Mountain air... Nothin' like it.

When his phone buzzed, he started and reached back to grab it from his pocket. He glanced at the screen at an unfamiliar number but answered it anyway.

"Moon."

"Um...Zayden?" The feminine voice had him leaping to his feet.

"Esme?"

"Yeah, it's me." Was she crying? He recognized that tightness in her tone and took off walking to his truck immediately.

"I was just calling to say I'm not lost on the mountain."

A groan lodged in his throat, unreleased. Something else was wrong—he could tell.

She continued, "I'm at the new steakhouse in town and I wondered if you'd like to join me."

Motherfucker. He yanked open his truck door. "What's going on?"

"Well, I'm standing here in a new dress and high heels, and I could use a date."

He slid into the truck and twisted the key in the ignition. "You're all dressed up and got no one to dance with?"

"Something like that."

"I'll be there in twenty."

Without waiting for her response, he ended the call and dropped his phone into the cup holder. Dammit. He'd bet everything he had left in the world that she'd been stood up by the same jerk who'd left her on the mountain. He pictured her now, standing in her new dress on the sidewalk out front of the steakhouse, waiting for a man who didn't deserve her time or attention.

He was getting ahead of himself. He didn't know it was the same guy—she could be dating again. But

95

unlikely if she'd been expecting a ring from the asshole.

If Zayden knew anything about women, it was how stubborn they could be when they found someone they believed was *the one.* Whether or not Esme fit into this box he wasn't certain, but she'd called him for help, and he had to go.

Minutes later, he pulled into the parking lot of the new steakhouse. The place once served as a slummy takeout joint, but they'd renovated the building, upgrading it with a log siding exterior, and the sign spoke of high-priced steaks that probably weren't worth what they charged for them.

He spotted her immediately, huddled in a long red coat that reached her slender calves. Below that, she balanced on heels that no woman could navigate the streets of Stokes wearing in February.

God, she'd gotten all dolled up for some asshole?

When his boots hit the sidewalk leading to the entry, she took a few steps toward him in her heels.

He raised a hand. "I'll come to you. You're liable to break your neck on this icy walkway." He hurried forward, gaze latched onto her face.

Her hair swirled in the breeze that wasn't as wild down here in town. As he approached, she gave him a smile full of false bravado.

"Thanks for meeting me on short notice. I've got a reservation for two." She turned to glance at the big doors carved with wilderness scenes of mountains and forest animals.

"You've got to be freezing, waiting out here." Drawing closer, he noticed the pink tinge to her nose and cheeks.

She buried her face in her coat collar. "I went inside and warmed up a couple times. Are you ready to go in?"

"Esme. What really happened?" No point in pretending everything was all right. He never was one to hide facts beneath a rainbow and call it gold — that was always Asher's job growing up.

She met his gaze, and he saw the pain glowing in those green eyes.

"You were meeting *him*, weren't you?" His voice came out gruff.

She nodded. "He said he wanted to take me out for a nice meal, that I deserved it. And he was going to explain his actions on Valentine's Day."

Jesus Christ. He hadn't believed her to be one of those ditzy chicks, but clearly he'd been wrong. "You bought that?"

She recoiled and drew herself up stiffly. "No. I did not buy that. I agreed to meet because I deserve some answers and an apology." He liked spunk in a woman — too much, in fact.

"You'll never get an apology from a prick like that."

"I see that now. But I do have dinner reservations, and I *am* wearing this new dress. So will you let me buy you a steak?"

He didn't have much money left in his pocket, and he still needed to give some of the earnings from the sale of the horse to the veterinarian, and somehow rustle up the cash to pay the fine he'd racked up. But he couldn't allow her to treat him to dinner either. He also didn't tell her he'd eaten hours ago, at Mimi's kitchen table.

He looked at her closely, seeing her worrying her lower lip with her teeth. "Do you really want to go in there now?"

She blinked. "What do you have in mind?"

He jerked his head. "Place down the road that's more my speed. Beer and pizza."

"I'm a little overdressed."

"You'll be perfect. What do ya say?" He waited for her to say no.

A soft smile spread over her lips and lit her eyes. She nodded. "Okay."

"Can you walk to my truck without falling on your face?"

"Of course." He heard a bit more strength in her voice.

As he led her to his vehicle, he couldn't help but try to puzzle out this woman, who put her blind trust into the wrong man twice but who had enough backbone to wander a mountain alone in a storm.

He opened the passenger door for her, and she looked up at him.

Hell. He didn't like that look. Actually, he did, but it was all wrong. "Yeah, I feel it too, but it isn't a date. It's two friends going out for pizza, all right?" He waved a hand for her to get in.

"Yes, exactly. Two friends." She climbed into his truck, and he closed the door.

When he settled beside her, he noted how she bundled the coat around her legs and wondered what was hidden beneath it. A short dress that would show off the curve of her ass?

He pulled out into the street and a couple minutes later, they were bumping into the parking lot of Pub Pizza.

"I can feel the bass of the music from here," she said.

He shot her a sideways grin. "Hope you can dance in those heels too."

"I'll take that challenge." Her wide smile lit her entire face, and damn if he didn't feel the aftereffects as he followed her out of the truck and up to the building.

The bass thumped, hitting deep in his chest. He opened the door for her. "I haven't torn up the town in a long time," he said.

She laughed. "Me either."

Inside, he glanced around for the best place to sit and have a drink, but it was a packed house. On the far side of the room, more than a dozen people danced to the fast tune, and he anticipated he knew more than one person in the joint. He only hoped they all steered clear of him.

"Moon."

Hell.

He glanced around to see a balding guy with a beer in each hand and the same snide expression he'd worn back in their high school days.

Zayden ignored him and closed his fingers around Esme's elbow. "Let's head up to the bar. Seems like the only place to sit."

She nodded and followed him. Behind him, he heard his name echoed again, this time from someone else. Great—the last thing he wanted were more fake-ass condolences over his father's demise, or any trouble either. And trouble seemed to follow him to places like this. What had he been thinking?

At the bar, he waited while Esme worked open the line of buttons on her coat. When the cloth parted to expose the sliver of a low neckline and the little black number, as well as her plump thighs, he battled no fewer than a dozen dirty ideas for how to wipe that ex of hers from her mind forever.

First, he'd set her on the bar and wrap those curls of hers around his fist, tipping her head back for his kiss, his tongue working down the dainty point of her jaw to her tantalizing cleavage…

Oblivious to the ravishing he was giving her in his mind, she removed her coat and folded it. Half the guys at the bar had twisted to stare at her. No wonder—she was the hottest thing in here, and those fuck-me shoes weren't helping a bit.

She hitched her round ass onto the stool and folded her coat across her lap. *Thank Christ—at least she's covered up.*

The bartender stopped before them. His smile was all for Esme. "Whattaya drinkin'?"

"I'll have tequila."

My kind of girl, Zayden thought, even as he was shaking his head.

"What do you mean no?" She narrowed her eyes at him.

"She means a double," he said to cover his action. "I'll have a draft."

The bartender moved off to fetch their drinks.

"I don't know if I can handle a double," she said over the music.

"Then don't drink it."

"I need something to make me forget what happened this evening."

I can think of a few things besides alcohol. He leaned closer to hear her and caught a whiff of her perfume. His cock stirred behind his fly.

Their drinks were placed before them, and too late he realized she hadn't eaten and was drinking on

101

an empty stomach. He pushed a basket of pretzels her way, and she nibbled one while he studied her.

Her curls cascaded over her shoulders, and some were trapped behind the shell of her ear. Two sets of gold hoops clung to her lobes. In the hollow of her throat, he watched her pulse flicker for a few beats before he tore his gaze away.

She tossed down half her drink and turned to him. "You wanna hit the dance floor?"

His lips quirked at one corner at the eagerness on her beautiful face. "Yeah, let's go."

She laid her coat over the barstool and swayed her hips as they cut through the crowd.

Hell, this was a terrible idea, but Zayden never shied away from a good mistake.

* * * * *

Everyone was watching Zayden, including her. Call it the tequila talking or her decision to have a good time after Owen stood her up, but she felt more and more infatuated by Zayden's hot body on the dance floor.

The man ground his hips, and she twisted around to present her own, knowing his gaze was latched onto her ass. He clamped his hands on her hips and swayed with her in time to the beat. When she felt his erection grind against her cheeks, a soft moan escaped her lips.

One hand wandered up her hip to knead her waist, shooting sparks of excitement through her. The song ended, and he whirled her to face him. Shamelessly, she hooked a thigh around his hard leg and rocked.

His gaze bore down into her, and she couldn't look away as they found the rhythm. The haze of alcohol began to dim after a half hour of dancing, but it felt as if the drops still worked through her empty stomach and fueled her actions.

Gripping his shirt front, she pulled him down 'til her lips reached ear level. "You're a good dancer."

He flashed a grin and twirled her, their bodies still touching so her breasts brushed his front, and then suddenly her back was plastered to his hard torso again. He wrapped his arms around her middle and tugged her back while thrusting his hips with hers.

Dear God, the man was smoking hot.

He was also a criminal, according to the ladies at work.

Well, she wasn't marrying him, so who cared?

When the music toned down to a slow song, she expected Zayden to take her into his arms, but instead he caught her hand and led her off the dance floor. At the bar, their drinks had been cleared, and her coat was slung over the end of the bar to make room for more patrons.

Zayden grabbed this and unfolded it for her.

Seeing he expected her to put the garment on, she slipped her arms into the sleeves and clutched the open front closed.

"Where are we doing?" she asked over the noise.

"Takin' you home." The hooded look he gave her carved a slick path of warmth through her lower belly and down between her legs.

Did he plan to get lucky? Did she want him to?

Outside, everything was covered in a fresh dusting of snow. The cool wind felt good on her hot face as they made their way to the truck. Zayden helped her inside, and she watched him circle the front.

By now, the alcohol burned out of her system, and she felt sober enough to realize that things could escalate between them. Her decent relationship with Owen ended terribly, resulting in her lack of trust. But she trusted Zayden.

We're just friends. He came to my rescue again, and he doesn't expect payment. We just danced.

Danced like we'd screwed a hundred times and knew just how to turn each other on.

Even being keyed up after all that, was she ready for more?

"Stop by the steakhouse so I can get my car," she said.

He swung into the parking lot and she remained seated a moment, looking at him. Was he thinking he should follow her home too?

She climbed out, and he followed, walking her to her vehicle. Standing next to her car, she looked up into his eyes.

He gave her that quirk of his lips she was coming to know so well. "You didn't get dinner. I'm sorry."

She shook her head. "I'm fine. Thank you for coming to my rescue a second time."

His smile vanished, and his expression intensified to that dark look she had seen on the dance floor. Her heart beat faster. She leaned in.

He did too...then he brushed his lips between her brows and stepped away. "You good to get home on your own?"

Surprise catapulted the last of her sexual fog out of her body as she realized he had no intention of coming home with her or taking things to another level.

She managed to nod.

"Good. See ya again sometime, Esme," he tossed over his shoulder as he returned to his truck and jumped behind the wheel.

For a moment, she didn't move. Was he rejecting her?

No, she hadn't asked for more than dinner. He'd given her dancing. Nobody mentioned sleeping together.

As she watched him drive off into the night, she could only shake her head. For all the rumors about

Zayden Moon, she sure didn't see that side of the man. To her, he was nothing but a gentleman.

Chapter Six

The noise of tires on gravel brought Zayden's attention from the saddle he was oiling, and he looked up toward the grimy barn window. Through it, the world remained but a blur. He'd need to take the polishing cloth to the glass next.

He dropped the cloth and walked out. Tugging his hat brim lower to shade his eyes from the blinding sun on snow, he spotted the unfamiliar truck coming to a halt in front of the house.

Might be one of Mimi's Ute relatives. If so, it was about time he met them.

After starting toward the vehicle in long strides, he was surprised when a tall man got out of the truck and turned his direction.

"Moon," the man said.

"Sorry, do I know you?" He drew up before the man.

"Knew you when you were a young'un."

That meant he knew his father, which couldn't be good. Anyone who claimed to be friends with Chaz Moon turned out to be a motherfucker just like their pa. And anyone else hated the man—and his sons by proxy.

Zayden hooked a thumb in the pocket of his jeans. "I'm Zayden. What can I do for ya?"

"Think we could go somewhere and sit down?"

He eyed the guy and couldn't see a single reason to make him more comfortable. "It's a nice day and looks like you spend too much time sitting as it is." He dropped his gaze to the man's paunchy stomach rolling over his gold belt buckle.

The man's brows shot up, but he composed himself. "All right then, I'll cut to the chase."

He waited.

"I belong to a coalition of local ranchers. Our goal is to stroke each other's backs when we can, by providing help if someone needs it, and that includes loaning money."

Ah, here it is.

Zayden wasn't going to make it easy on the guy and offered no encouragement to continue.

"About five years back, your father came to us looking for aid. He was at the end of his funds and about to lose the ranch. We pooled together and offered him a private loan, to be paid back in—"

"Lemme guess—five years," Zayden cut across him.

He nodded.

"Am I supposed to believe this? I haven't seen any paperwork or proof of a private loan debt." He hadn't exactly gotten around to digging through his father's boxes of junk, where it could be hidden, either. But he had to be cautious—lots of scams happened after people died.

"I've got the papers here in my truck. Let me get them." He turned to his vehicle again and fished around inside. When he returned with a couple sheets in hand, he gave Zayden a hard look, which he returned. He'd sized up better men than this one, and he wasn't going to be cowed because the guy had known him when he was a young'un.

Zayden glanced at the paper and back at him. "Is this legally filed anywhere?"

"You can see right here that your father's name is listed as the borrower." He poked a thick finger at the page.

Zayden gave him a bland look. "I can read, thanks. What I'm asking is how do I know you didn't cook up a scheme to wring money from me after my old man died, and this is a falsified document?"

"The others in the coalition can vouch for it. Every one of our signatures is there."

Skimming the paper again, he saw one number with too many zeroes behind it.

Ten grand. The old man owed ten grand? If he'd borrowed that amount years ago, no evidence existed it had been put to good use. The buildings needed work. No new equipment was stashed away in the garage. Which meant he either drank it up or actually purchased items for the ranch, which he later sold.

Mimi might know something, and he would ask as soon as he got this jackass back into his truck and off his property.

"I'll call my lawyer," he said, brushing past the man on his way to the house.

He didn't bother to glance back to see if the guy was leaving, but he heard the engine start and then the crunch of tires again.

Walking into the house, he glared at the papers he held. Then he slammed the door behind himself and read them proper. No less than ten other ranchers, most names he recognized as lifers in these parts, had signed the document, and so had his stupid father.

Groaning, he walked into the living room. In the bright sun of the day, everything looked shabbier and he was beginning to think it would all look better as ash after he burned it to the ground.

The old desk stood along one wall. Their father always warned him and his brothers to stay out of the drawers, and they were scared enough of him that they obeyed. But dear old pops was dead, and no wonder if he'd pickled his liver with ten thousand dollars' worth of booze.

When he opened the bottom drawer, several bottles clinked as they rolled to the front. Disgust twisted his lips. He thought he'd purged all the empty whiskey bottles in the house, but he had a feeling he'd be finding them for years to come — if he stuck around.

He tossed these on the carpet and dug out the rest of the drawer's contents. After ten minutes, all he found was garbage. Junk receipts from two decades ago for things like oil filters and spark plugs. Back when their dad gave a crap about keeping things up.

After working his way through two more drawers, he lit upon a file folder. When he flipped it open and saw the matching paper the rancher had given him, Zayden released the angry growl he'd been holding back.

"Oh dear. Was that man who was here Frank Branch?"

He looked up at Mimi's frail voice.

"Didn't catch his name."

"I thought I recognized him, but my eyes are old and I wasn't entirely sure." Dropping her attention to the folder Zayden held, she nodded. "He was here to collect on the loan, wasn't he?"

"I'm not surprised you knew about it. Nothing gets past you, Mimi." He sighed and tossed the folder onto the desk, then rubbed a sore spot between his eyes where a headache began to form. "How much more debt is there, Mimi? Do you have any idea?"

"Your father only took the loan from the coalition to try to get a fresh start." Was she defending the drunk bastard?

Zayden pushed out a rough laugh. "I see it worked. That ten grand fixed up the house"—he waved a hand at their worn surroundings—"and the barn. Hell, that herd of healthy cattle is testament to my father's good business sense." He kicked one of the bottles at his feet, and it struck the other with a loud *clank*.

"You've got a right to be angry, Zayden. Your father didn't do right by any of you, but a few years ago, he saw that for himself. He woke up one day and realized his boys didn't come home or want anything to do with him, so he decided to get clean, stop drinking and make this ranch something again."

"Looks like he did a fine job o' that. All he left us with—*me* with—is bills and debt and no way to keep this place afloat, let alone profitable."

He moved his stare from the threadbare carpet to the battered furniture that had borne the brunt of more than one of Chaz Moon's fits of anger.

"How have you been managing all these years, Mimi?"

The woman's age appeared on her face when she met his gaze. "It hasn't been easy. I have a bit of money I inherited from my mother's family. And my Ute relatives always help when they can, even if it's to bring me a haunch of venison. I also do some sewing work for people in town, and that provides a bit of pocket money."

"In other words, you're funding this ranch, and my deadbeat father took advantage of you all those years. Jesus." He tore off his hat and scrubbed a hand over his face. Just when he thought he couldn't hate the son of a bitch more, he discovered another good reason to.

"I'm not sure you boys ever understood."

"Understood what, Mimi?"

"This ranch is my home too."

The lump in his throat was too hard to swallow, but he got it down as he stepped up to take her in his arms. She hugged him back, patting him the way she always did.

"You're tough, Zayden. You did things at a young age that no boys ever should have to, but you did it without complaint. You hired the ranch hands. You paid them in cash. You organized cattle sales and hired me to come here and help you all." She turned teary blue eyes on him. "I like to think you're the true owner of Moon Ranch, and now it's going to take some digging to get out of the hole we're in. But it's not impossible, boy."

He gave her a sarcastic grin. "Isn't it?"

She stepped away. "Not with your drive and determination."

"You aren't just saying this because you don't want to leave the ranch? That you have nowhere else to go?" It hurt him to think of Mimi on her own here all these years. How selfish he'd been to not see her cared for before taking off.

She smiled, a real one compared to his moments ago. "I can leave anytime I want. Like I said, there's a small amount of money from my mother's side, and it's enough for me to have an apartment in town. And my great-nephew's been asking me for years to come live with him and his family. They don't like the thought of me down here alone."

He stared at her for a long minute. "Christ, how did you ever put up with my father? Or any of us, for that matter? We weren't the best kids growing up, always in trouble in school and sometimes with the law."

Reaching up, she cupped his jaw like a mother would a son's. She searched his eyes. "Don't you know? It's because I love ya, boy. I love all of ya, and I would have laid down my life for you if necessary."

"Thank God it never came to that." He shook his head, and she dropped her hand from his face. "You're the best, Mimi. I'm sorry for so much."

"Time to turn that corner, Zayden. Take what's yours and make it right again." The power in her voice lifted him on a sail of hope.

But the sensation was fleeting, because he still had a hell of a lot of debt and decisions to make.

"Remember that side business you and your brothers had going when you were fifteen?" she asked.

He scuffed his knuckles over his jaw. "The tree cutting service?"

"Yes. I've heard a few people in town could use some work done on their properties. The old neighbor up the road too—Sutton. Maybe it's time to sharpen that old chainsaw in the garage." With that, she returned to the kitchen, to do whatever Mimi did to pass the time.

He wandered to the window and gazed at the white world outside. February wasn't an ideal time to start up a tree trimming service, but plenty of people still needed firewood cut at this time of year, especially when their wood-burning stoves were devouring logs as fast as they could feed them to keep the house warm.

Having a small income and side work would take some of the load off Mimi, and she could start using her money in ways beyond pouring it down the money pit of this ranch.

If he got that equity loan too, he'd be able to pay off the ranchers coalition and the vet, but the amount of money he needed to give this ranch the boost it needed wouldn't stretch that far.

First things first. He drove to the Suttons and offered his services. The older man remembered him and his brothers and showed him right to a pair of pines overhanging the house roof that he feared would fall under the weight of the snow, and it was late in the season for such work, but did Zayden think he could cut them without much trouble?

Eyeing the leaning trunks and the angles over the roof, he said, "You got a tractor and some chains to put tension on the trees so they fall in the other direction?"

Sutton nodded. "Be happy to do it."

"Today?" He eyed the man.

"No time like the present."

Zayden walked around the trunks, assessing the angles and where to place the cuts. "Do you want the wood cut up afterward?"

"Don't have need of it. We use a pellet stove for heating the house. But if you could use it, you're welcome to carry it off."

He could sell it. Being fresh cut, it wouldn't be useful for burning this season, but people bought wood to stockpile for later in the year. "I'll clear it away for you. The branches too." Pines were a mess to clean up, but hard work never killed anybody.

"I appreciate your offer. So we have a deal. Three hundred for each tree."

It was worth much more, but Zayden would take anything at this point. He tugged the brim of his hat. "Yes, sir."

The man looked at him for several heartbeats. Zayden hoped he didn't give him the I'm-sorry-about-your-father spiel, because he was getting sick of hearing it.

"You know, I don't blame you boys for not stickin' around or showing up to visit your father all those years."

Dragging in a deep breath, he battled some of the dormant anger he would forever possess when it came to his upbringing. All he could do was take Mimi's advice to turn a new leaf and set things right.

When he didn't respond, the man continued, "We all knew Moon was a bastard."

"At least we agree on that," he said.

Sutton flashed a grin, showing off pearly white dentures. "I'll get the tractor, boy, and we'll get to work."

"You need any help?"

"With the chains, yeah. They're heavy, and I'm not as tough as I used to be." He took off walking toward the big outbuilding housing the tractor. He tossed a look over his shoulder at Zayden. "But you've still got the whole world in front of you, son."

Zayden's chest welled with emotion. *Yeah, I do.* And he wasn't going to pass up the chance to use his brains, skills, and hell, even that Moon charm, if it meant getting the ranch off the ground again.

* * * * *

Esme narrowed her eyes onto the backside of the man standing in the yard across the street. That

117

cowboy hat, the set of his shoulders were all too familiar.

Zayden.

She hadn't seen the man since their encounter, but the urge in her gut to put on her boots and go outside to talk to him proved stronger than any shyness she might have. When she started across the street, the homeowner came out to talk to Zayden.

She listened a moment as they exchanged words about the broken tree in the man's yard.

"You think you can take it down, even with the snow and such?" the man asked.

Zayden gave a nod, peering up at the trunk that had snapped under the weight of an early storm. "I can do it."

"Good. We agreed on a hundred fifty, right?"

Zayden eyed him. "That's a bit on the low side. That's cleanup too."

"I know others who'll do the same work for less."

"I can't do it for that. I've got my own work to see to." Zayden eyed the man and then caught sight of her from the corner of his eye. He turned his head and pierced her with his stare.

Too late to go back inside now that she was spotted, she ventured over to him. "Hi Zayden. You keeping busy with work here in town now?"

He nodded. "That's right."

"I wondered when these townspeople would get you to come and do their work—I know how much they demand your services all over the countryside. You did that work up on State Ranch, didn't you?" Her lies fell off her lips like gumdrops.

The corner of his mouth twitched, but he didn't let on that she was making this all up. Meanwhile, the homeowner listened to the exchange.

She turned her eyes on the man. "You know you've got the absolute best right in front of you, don't you?"

The man hesitated. "I guess I do."

She pivoted to Zayden again. "I heard you only charged five hundred for slicing up that fallen tree at the Cauffman's."

This time Zayden's lips did quirk upward, his eyes glimmering with amusement. "Well, I had to cut them a deal, since I'll be trimming the rest of the trees on their property come spring."

She smiled. "If you're looking for more work today, I know someone who comes into the credit union. He was saying—"

"Three hundred," the homeowner interjected.

Zayden gave him his attention. They stared at each other for a long moment.

"Three-fifty." Zayden's gruff tone sent a shiver shooting through Esme's body, and she wrapped her arms around herself.

"Deal. Get started today and make sure you get all the little sticks in the yard."

Zayden pulled his hat brim. "Will do. I'll get my saw."

The homeowner shook his head and went into the house, leaving them standing alone.

"I'm dyin' to know where all that came from," Zayden drawled.

She grinned. "Just helping out a friend. You deserved more than a hundred and fifty dollars."

"I appreciate you stepping in. But who the hell are the Cauffmans?"

She burst out laughing, and he added his deep chuckles to it. When their gazes locked, that deep shiver took hold of her stomach, telling her that the attraction she felt wasn't something she was imagining. The dark expression in his eyes spoke way more.

He stood there another long moment, staring at her. "You'd best get back home before you freeze out here."

"All right. See ya around, Zayden."

"Bye, sweetheart."

As she crossed the street again, she felt a heavy weight of eyes on her back and put a little extra sway into her hips. Moments later, she heard the saw start up and went to the window to peek out at the gorgeous hunk of a cowboy cutting up wood.

He was a hard worker. Reliable. And dang if she didn't want to see much more of him.

* * * * *

Cleaning up the tree took two long days, but he'd finally finished. As Zayden settled behind the wheel of his truck, he glanced up and down the side street of Stokes. Most of the businesses were on the main strip, and it had grown a lot since he'd left. Also, some of the smaller ma and pop businesses had vanished, replaced by pricier and more commercialized convenience stores and hardware stores. Still, the town boasted a quaintness that would probably never change, and for that he was glad.

He started the engine, but continued to sit there a moment. He thought of Esme's appearance and how she'd lied through her pretty white teeth to get that homeowner to pay him more for his services. The woman had a way about her that reached out and grabbed a man, and she'd worked a miracle with that guy. And to think people called him a charmer.

He sat another moment, drinking in the scenery in front of him. With a small wad of bills in his pocket, it was easy to think of the now and consider taking Esme out on the town tonight. But that was how he'd blown every paycheck the past decade, and other things took precedence this time.

At least he didn't blow every dime on booze, like his father. He'd broken that chain.

Leaning forward, he dug a long forefinger around in the ashtray of the old truck and touched metal. He fished out the large flat disk as big as a silver dollar and stared at the words engraved on it. He'd found the piece in his father's desk after rooting around to get to the bottom of what was owed, and he'd been shocked to see his father, at some point, had gone through the Alcoholics Anonymous 12-step program.

He'd achieved a 30-day coin. The words *To Thine Own Self Be True,* had resonated with more shock in Zayden, because for the first time ever, he didn't know who the hell his father really was.

Sure, he knew the man as a drunk. But deep down, there must have been more to Chaz Moon. He had once been someone's son and lover. He had been a child who laughed and played with toys.

Neither Zayden nor his brothers had ever seen this side of their dad, but during those thirty days of sobriety, he wasn't drunk. Had he been different?

Zayden hadn't gotten up the gumption to ask Mimi about it yet, but he would. He tossed the coin back into its hiding spot and looked up and down the street before pulling out.

When he drove past the credit union, he considered stopping again to see how things were progressing with the equity loan. Was it normal to take so long? They needed proof of the ranch changing hands in addition to the regular credit checks, and that took time, he supposed.

But right now he didn't care much about the money—his thoughts centered on Esme.

The woman had made a couple cameo appearances in his dreams, and every time he drove into Stokes, he wondered if he'd run into her.

Besides the previous day, he never did, but she haunted him for hours afterward. Hell, she was haunting him now.

Having a woman was a natural progression of life, wasn't it? No. No, it wasn't. Not for him. He wasn't normal, and he had nothing to offer but a lot of misery to come.

He slowed as he approached a red light. When he laid eyes on the woman walking along the sidewalk, he slowed to a crawl. He knew those curls. He'd wrapped them in his hands in his dreams.

Pulling up abreast of her, he rolled down the window. "You headed out to meet some jackass?"

Her head jerked around. To soften his words, he gave her a crooked smile.

She pierced him with her gaze, and a smile spread over her face. "Actually no. I'm taking a long break to have a teeth cleaning." She wore a shorter black coat today, as well as black pants. Damn if they didn't hug her ass perfectly.

"Beware of dentists. Never agree to the laughing gas. You never know what they'll do to you while you're under."

She giggled. "I'll remember that."

He parked the truck to let a few cars pass. "You're walking?"

"It's only a few blocks, and it's a nice day."

He dropped his gaze to her footwear. She wore boots that encased her calves, and fur peeped from the tops.

"Want a ride?" His mind asked if this was a wise move on his part, and he kicked that voice of reason aside and told it to shut up. He wasn't asking her to go out with him and add him to her list of jackasses she'd dated — it was only a ride.

"Get in," he said.

She hesitated and then opened the door and slid inside. He rolled up the window for her, and they shared a long look that roused all the memories of his dreams.

"How have you been?" he asked.

"Fine. No new adventures to report."

He cocked a brow. "Haven't been swindling any neighbors?"

Her eyes twinkled. "I've just been working."

"Me too."

She looked at him closer. "You're covered in sawdust and the whole truck smells like a pine tree."

He chuckled. "I just finished up that guy's tree. It took longer than I hoped."

"Isn't it odd to do that sort of work in February?"

"You'd be surprised how many people have trees that need cutting after the last few storms, for safety reasons. I'll pick up more work once spring breaks, I'm sure."

"So, this is your job now?"

He paused, studying her face. Her earnest expression conveyed so much interest, he found it hard to remember why he didn't normally talk openly to people.

"I've got the ranch since my dad passed. But it's a work in progress."

"I'm sure there's always hard work to do."

"Yeah, and things are tight right now, so I've been doing odd jobs to make ends meet." He sounded like the worst catch in Colorado. Hell, no surprise there. He was. The only man worse had just been buried.

"I think that's great," she said.

"Yeah, it's great," he echoed.

"I'm not being sarcastic, Zayden." Her brows crinkled. "I'm serious. Any work is good work. Plus...you smell good."

His mouth quirked up. "That fresh pine scent always gets the ladies. That's actually my reason for doing this. I just didn't want to sound like a player."

She laughed, curls bouncing around her face, and he had a sudden urge to lightly pinch the point of her chin between his fingers, lean in and kiss her.

Suddenly, she sobered, an intense glow lighting her green eyes. He'd noticed those freckles on her nose before, while warming her in sleep. He'd examined every inch of her by sight and feel, and what he didn't know, his dreams had filled in the blanks.

Pink settled in her cheeks, and she darted her tongue over her lips. "It's great seeing you, but I really do need to make that dentist appointment. I have to return to work afterward."

He pulled into the road again and went three more blocks 'til she pointed out a building painted dark green. He parked out front and turned to her.

"Stay out of trouble, Esme."

She smiled softly. "I will. You too, Zayden."

He grinned. "Not likely, but I'll do my best."

For a long heartbeat, she remained seated, staring at him. He locked his gaze on hers, and damn if there wasn't a spark there.

Hell... he couldn't let her make another mistake in him.

"I've gotta get back to the ranch too. See ya again sometime."

She nodded and reached for the door handle. He watched her get out, wishing he could be like a normal guy who just asked out a woman he was interested in, but he was better off.

And so was she.

Chapter Seven

Why, oh why, had Esme let Natalie talk her into trying an online dating service? More than a month had passed since Owen stood her up at the steakhouse, and well...it seemed like a good idea at the time.

Now she sat here stuck with this asshole who loved with his own hair more than anything else, and who thought she owed him something because he'd bought her two drinks. Could she really be ready to move on from Owen? The answer to that—yes. She no longer cared about his reasons for leaving her on the mountain or standing her up at the steakhouse. Bottom line, he didn't want her, and she was worth more than he ever would deserve.

But putting herself back in the dating scene made her question the decision, especially when scraping the bottom of the barrel. And to think this guy appeared to be the best of three options to fill her Friday night.

As she pretended to listen to him drone on about his achievements, her mind wandered to Zayden Moon. Seeing him again had been a surprise, and one that had left her feeling both breathless and bent out of shape for a long time afterward. Now, almost a week later, he still hadn't been back into the credit union, and she couldn't find a good enough reason for calling him out of the blue, either.

Yet she thought about him—a lot.

While her date continued his one-sided conversation about how he got his hair barbered weekly, when most men tidied themselves up every six weeks, she considered having another adult beverage. But if she wanted to drive home from this disastrous date, that was out of the question.

He stared at her cleavage, and she shifted to detract attention from her assets. What a bad choice of tops to wear on a first date, and again, she blamed Natalie, because when asked, the woman had chosen it out of a half dozen options.

"So, what do you say about going back to my place for a nightcap?" He ran his tongue over his lips.

"I don't think that's a good idea. We only just met."

"But you're enjoying yourself. Why not continue the enjoyment…in private?"

She opened her mouth to tell him she was leaving, and thankfully her phone rang in the depths of her handbag. "Excuse me," she said smoothly to her date and got up from the table to take the call in private. To be on the safe side, she took her coat and purse with her.

Without looking at the screen, she knew it was Natalie checking in on her, as Esme had made her promise to do. Boy, was her coworker in for an earful.

"Natalie, you soooo owe me after this. I don't know why I let you talk me into going out, because this guy's a—"

"Esme, it's me. Owen." His slurred words told her immediately he was drunk-calling.

Why had she forgotten to block his number? That was next on her agenda, right after she got rid of him and ditched her date too.

She made a beeline for the exit. Phone pressed hard to her ear, she said, "Owen, you have no business calling me."

"Don't be like that, Esme. We had such great times together. Remember that little red number you wore that night? I still love you, baby."

"You're drunk. And you're a dick."

"You want a dick pic? Ohhh yeah, you always liked mine. Hold on."

To her horror, the phone buzzed with a text before she could end the call. Sure enough, the photo popped up on her screen.

She clapped the phone to her ear again. "Owen, you're a pathetic waste-oid, and your dick pic makes me puke in my mouth. Don't try to contact me again—I'm blocking you."

She ended the call, breathing hard with disgust and anger. Then she deleted the photo from her phone and blocked his number.

Meanwhile, her date was still waiting for her to return.

Screw him too. Let him go to bed with his hair clippers.

She headed toward her car in the parking lot. She needed to blow off some steam, have a nice rant. But Natalie would only giggle at her trials and tribulations, and right now, she wanted somebody to get angry on her behalf.

Before she knew her own mind, she was dialing Zayden's number.

He answered after one ring. "Esme?"

"It's me." A beat of silence hung between them.

"Everything all right?" His gruff tone brought his image into her mind's eye. The rugged set of his features, his dark eyes. And all that *fiiiiine* muscle. The scent of pine wood chips floated in the back of her nose.

"Not exactly. I'm on a date."

"Tell me it's not with your ex."

"No. But that jerk just called *and* sent me a dick pic."

"Jesus Christ."

"I blocked him. But the date thinks I owe him something."

"Like hell."

"I know. I'm not calling for you to rescue me—again. I only wanted to talk to a man who knows how a woman should be treated."

A long beat of silence passed.

She swallowed. Maybe it was the wrong idea to call Zayden.

"I just wondered what it is about me that makes guys turn into complete assholes when they're around me? Am I one of those girls that guys love to mistreat?" Her question blurted from her lips as if she'd drank far more than the two small cocktails back in the restaurant.

Zayden sighed heavily into her ear. "Why do you keep doing this to yourself? You're worth more."

Without words for her own defense, she could only burn about her choices. But she could fix that. Starting now, she was turning her back on assholes.

"Where are you right now?" Zayden asked.

"Ronaldos."

"Meet me at the Pub Pizza again, but don't go inside—wait for me in the parking lot. I'm coming."

Like last time, Zayden ended the call without even a goodbye. She cradled her phone and stared at it. He was...coming? To meet her?

For a moment, she had no idea what to do. Call him back and tell him not to bother? What if she really wanted to see him, though?

Whether she met him or not, she definitely needed to get away from this place, before her date realized she wasn't coming back and came looking for her. At least the man lived out of town and he didn't use the credit union for his finances, so she never had to set eyes on him again.

It was time to put that man in her past, and she couldn't peal out faster. She started her car and stepped on the gas, tearing out of the parking lot of the restaurant, and headed to the Pub Pizza.

When she reached the place, she parked and sat in the dark, waiting for Zayden to pull in.

What would she say to him?

Only a few minutes later, her heart clenched to see the old truck bumping into the lot. He parked beside her and climbed out. Even in the dark, the sight of his sexy body made hers fire on all cylinders.

She reached for the door handle, but he slid into her passenger seat. Huge, gorgeous, sucking all the air out of the car and raising her internal temperature about a hundred degrees.

He raked his gaze over her, taking in her hair and face, then working down the coat she'd thrown on and landing on her legs in her skirt and pantyhose.

"Bad date?" he asked.

She nodded.

"So you called to tell me about yet another asshole treating you bad."

She dropped her head. "When you put it that way, I sound like more of an idiot than I already feel like."

He made a noise, low in his throat. Slowly, he reached out and cupped her face. The strength and warmth of his hand made her burn for more of his touch.

"You go out with these jackasses and then call me when it all goes wrong. Are you seeing a pattern?"

She didn't realize she had been doing that, but she couldn't deny she'd used Zayden.

"You pick all the wrong guys," he stated.

She shivered as he ran the pad of his thumb across her lips.

His voice sounded rough. "Let me show you how it's done." His low words smeared across her soul, and she felt herself leaning toward him.

He lowered his head in increments, his gaze latched to her lips. She wet them, and he growled.

"You don't want to get mixed up with me," he said.

"It's just for sex."

When his crooked grin hit his handsome face, she laughed, low.

"It's not the worst decision I've made tonight to take you home with me." She tipped her face up to his, almost begging for his hard lips on hers.

"Am I sensing some revenge sex here? If that's the case, I'm your guy. I can show these assholes what they've lost." Zayden moved in, a breath away from nuzzling her just like she wanted.

Her heart slammed against her chest, and she could barely drag in a full breath, especially with him filling the car with his masculine scent.

She nodded, rubbing her nose against his. "Maybe."

"Then let's do it right, sweetheart." Suddenly, he released her, and she slumped in her seat, panting with want. "Drive."

* * * * *

Thank God that Esme's house wasn't far, because he was hard as steel and aching to glide into that curvy body of hers.

When he'd gotten the call from her, he'd been sitting in the dark living room, fantasizing about having her beneath him anyway. So fate brought them together, and now there was no stopping him from showing Esme just how she deserved to feel with a man.

God, her thighs drove him nuts. He had ten visions of parting them and diving into that dark shadow between them before she pulled up in front of her house.

He got out and shot around the car before she completely gained her feet. He grabbed her under the round globes of her ass and lifted her against him.

She moaned, and their mouths connected. He thrust his tongue between her soft warm lips

135

gathering more of her sweetness, all before he kicked her car door shut.

"Take me to bed, cowboy," she murmured against his lips.

He bit into her plump lower lip and tugged. "Hang on to me."

She slid her arms around his neck, and he lifted her. She hooked her thighs around his hips as he walked to the front door. Her skirt rode up, and the liquid heat from her center bumped against his erection with every excruciatingly slow step.

Need created a harsh blast of flames, and she fumbled with the key and front door before they stumbled inside.

They took one look at each other, and it was game on.

She started tearing at his shirt buttons, and he held the curves of her ass in his hands, kneading her soft globes as he captured her mouth again. This time, she kissed him back with all the fervor he needed to get him harder than he'd ever been in his life.

Her cool fingers found skin where she'd opened his shirt, and she explored his pec. When her fingertip brushed his nipple, he groaned and let her slide down his body till her feet hit the floor.

She kicked off her high heels, dropping her a few inches in height. The glow of her eyes displayed unmistakable desire.

His hands hovered over her—and in one swift jerk, he ripped the red coat off her. It crumpled at their feet.

"Zayden…" It came as a soft plea.

"Fuck yeah." He lashed an arm around her middle and yanked her off her feet again, carrying her a few steps to the sofa in the middle of the room. They collapsed to it in a tangle of tongues. He tugged her skirt all the way over her hips so it became a wad of fabric around her waist. Under her pantyhose, he discovered she wore a nude-colored thong, and he almost lost it.

Esme finished with his shirt buttons so the garment hung all the way open, and she leaned back to look at him. Her gaze traveled over his chest to his abs and downward to encompass the bulge in his jeans.

His cock throbbed.

Reaching for her hair, he pulled whatever pins held the wild mass in place. All he wanted were the unruly curls brushing his skin when he sank his dick inside her.

She moved in for another kiss, gliding her hands in the open flaps of his shirt and removing it from his shoulders. He bracketed her face with his hands and angled her where he wanted for the deepest, dirtiest kiss ever.

God, the woman was a wild one, and he was barely holding back from flipping her over and plunging into her.

He grabbed her hair in one fist and twisted his mouth free of hers to latch it onto her throat. She cried out. He sucked lightly and released her again, moving down the column scented by perfume, to her collarbone. He kissed along it and then jerked her top over her head.

Her curls bounced. Her breasts bounced. And he had to get her completely naked — now.

As this thought hit, she went for his belt buckle, and the girl knew how to undress a man, her touch tormenting him to the point of blowing. When her fingertips brushed his fly, he put an end to her teasing.

He tossed her back on the sofa, and she grinned.

"How do I get this skirt off?"

"There's a zipper on the back," she panted.

"Fuck." He flipped her face-down, and she shook with giggles as he worked the cloth back down from her waist, over her hips, and then unzipped it and ripped the garment from her body.

He paused to look at her. In only a bra and that sexy thong, with her pantyhose still intact, the view from the back was something to see.

She turned her face from the couch cushion to look at him. "You perving on me, Zayden?"

"Oh yeah. You have no idea how hot your ass looks in those pantyhose." He delivered a slap to her backside.

She squealed and flipped over. She wiped her hair away from her cheeks, eyes burning up into his and a grin on her beautiful face.

He braced his elbows on the narrow sofa around her and leaned in to claim her mouth. Soft cries escaped her as she explored his body with her fluttery touch. Need blasted like dynamite through him, and he felt his balls draw up in preparation.

"Don't make me beg," she whispered between long passes of his tongue over hers.

He flashed a grin. "I never do anything halfway." He popped the clasp of her bra, freeing her round tits.

* * * * *

Her nipples throbbed beneath his stare, and she arched upward, urging him to take one of the needy buds into his mouth—between his teeth...anything to ease this ache inside her.

For what felt like a full minute, he skated his gaze over her, drinking in her face, her hair, her breasts and lower to her thong, now soaked with desire.

She looked at him too. She'd never seen such a beautiful man outside of photos. He was carved in all the right places, his abs ridged to his belt that hung open.

Urging him to suck her nipples, she cupped her breasts together in offering. She'd never been so wanton, but there wasn't anything to lose, and Zayden was a once in a lifetime opportunity.

When he groaned and lapped at one of her straining buds, she focused on the scalding feel of his tongue.

"Hold them just like that for me. Hell, you're delicious." He licked her nipple again and again, then moved to the other. This one he took in the heat of his mouth, and she bucked with a cry.

He grazed his teeth over the tip and nibbled before releasing it and turning to the other for the same attention. She flung her head back and succumbed to sensation. His mouth moving over her breasts, sucking and biting her into a frenzy, was just what she needed to feel like a desirable woman... To feel alive.

As he raised his head, she clasped his nape and realized somewhere in the flurry of stripping each other, he'd lost his hat. The longish strands of his hair felt soft under her fingers, and she twisted them, dragging him back down to her breasts again.

"You haven't been kissed this way in a long time, have you, sweetheart?"

She shook her head, but he wasn't paying attention, because he moved lower on her body. Between her breasts, he placed a line of kisses all the way to her navel.

He dragged his rough, angular jaw over her skin till it prickled. But when he hooked his fingers in her pantyhose and eased them from her body with exquisite and mind-blowing slowness, her chest heaved for air.

His eyes bore into hers. "Ready for this?"

"For what?" Her voice wasn't her own.

"For the best pussy eating you've ever had in your life?"

Dear. God. Yes.

The next second, her pussy was bared, her thong shredded right off her body.

Zayden ducked his head to her pulsating center and parted his lips over her pussy. She shook in the grasp of his hands on her hips. As he slipped his warm, wet tongue over her seam and circled her clit, she spread her legs wide and cried out.

When he said the best pussy eating she ever had in her life, he meant it. The man should win an award. *He should... he should...* She sucked in sharply... *keep going.*

Each flip of his tongue through her drenched folds caused her to spike higher and higher. The need to have him filling her made her inner walls clench. He dragged his tongue down through her slick heat to her opening. He circled it once and then dived in.

With his hands on her thighs, pressing them wider apart, she gave him full access by lifting her ass off the sofa. Hell, she'd serve herself up with a side of blow job as long as he got her to the blissful finale.

Her thighs shook, and he poured attention into his task, coaxing more cries from her lips that soon became guttural moans. He tongue-lashed her channel, somehow finding a spot that tipped the scales even more harshly toward the end in sight.

Grinding her hips, she pushed her pussy into his face and begged for the pleasure he was so good at giving. He opened his mouth wide, resting his upper lip on her bundle of nerves as he tongued her.

"Oh my God," she squeaked, no air left in her lungs.

He rumbled against her soaking flesh, and it was all over. Her orgasm hit hard, with a blinding explosion she couldn't see or think through.

* * * * *

While she pulsated on his tongue, he gathered her sweet juices and allowed himself a moment of need so fucking strong and powerful that he didn't know how to harness it.

He savored her another moment, teasing her before lifting his mouth from her drenched core.

Jesus, one look at her splayed wide for him and he was tearing open his jeans, shoving them down his hips. He kicked off his boots and shimmied out of everything before realizing he needed a condom.

With a growl of impatience, he located one in his wallet. He shoved it to the base of his erection and hovered over her, looking into her eyes.

Her hair created a cloud around her face, her eyes big and hazed with passion. Her lips swollen, bitten even.

Hell, she was begging him with those green eyes of hers, and how could he resist?

He fucking couldn't, and there was no reason to.

In one hard jerk, he filled her with his cock. Her slippery heat enveloped him, and he closed his eyes on a growl. The points of her nails dug into his shoulders, and he covered her with his body, mouth moving with hers as he withdrew nice and slow.

Her breath hitched. He was about to shatter.

Since that first night on the mountain when she'd been in his arms, he'd wanted her. Then again when she'd ground her ass against him on the dancefloor. Just having her beside him in the truck that day he'd picked her up on her way to an appointment had been a battle of wills to keep from touching her.

The call tonight sent him over the edge and he knew there was no use in holding back — there was an animal fire between them, and he had to have a taste or die trying.

He buried himself again, balls deep. She wrapped her arms around him tighter, moving with his every thrust as they galloped too damn fast toward the finish line.

Taking a woman this way was outside his norm. He usually got in and out just to satisfy his needs. But when she curled around him, mouth to his ear, and shook with her next orgasm, he floundered through some turbulent waters of the unknown.

She was fun and easy to talk to. Sexy as hell and even naughty enough at times to make him want to see more. So much more...

His release rushed up, tearing through him till his cock erupted with a harsh blow that stole his breath. He buried his face in her sweet neck and churned his hips through the ecstasy.

The haze went on for what felt like an hour. Dammit.

He rolled off the couch with her onto the floor, and she giggled as she curled up in his arms. Her hair pooled over his chest and shoulder, and he closed his eyes at the soft feel. Gently, she traced a fingertip over his pecs and down his abs.

When she shifted, he flexed his arm to hold her in place.

That couldn't be good—the first step toward getting far too wrapped up, something he'd sworn not to do.

He and relationships were fire and gasoline. His upbringing ensured he was a fucked-up mess for whatever woman tried to get him to commit, and engaging in late-night sex and living fast and loose were his style.

He may have enjoyed giving Esme enough pleasure to curl her hair tighter, but she didn't need another jerk in her life.

She came to me. She called me.

He liked being the hero in her life, the man she needed when feeling low, and that scared the hell out of him. The messed-up thinking was probably yet another byproduct of his childhood. He played the role of the fixer—always had. She called, and he ran to her when he should have walked away. Instead, he'd stripped her and fucked her good.

When she rolled atop him, plastering all those damp curves to his body, he sucked in a deep breath. He was already starting to lose his mind a second time.

She smiled, the soft bow of her lips accompanied by an undeniable warmth in her eyes. "I think you did it, Zayden."

"What's that?"

"Exorcised my demons. After that, I can't even remember my exes' names."

He rumbled a laugh and stroked her spine. She shivered in the wake of his touch, and he couldn't stop himself from brushing a kiss over her lips. For now, he wouldn't overthink things. He had a naked woman sprawled atop him, and he wouldn't waste the opportunity.

"I have more condoms," she whispered in his ear. "In my bedroom."

In a flash, he lifted her in his arms bridal style and moved through her dark house to find that bed.

Chapter Eight

Monday afternoon at work, Esme still couldn't shake her brain back down from the cloud that Zayden put it on. She had to count her money drawer twice to correct her error, and it was all the sexy cowboy's fault.

The man had done more than give her the best sex of her life—he'd burrowed into her psyche, and she could hardly think of anything *but* him.

After doing his best to use up every last condom in her nightstand drawer, he'd chosen to leave her in the middle of the night. Though she'd been deprived of sleeping in his arms like she had on the mountain, he'd departed in the best possible way. Leaning over her, kissing her softly, telling her to get some rest and he'd text her in the morning, which he had.

He'd said all the right things too, leaving them on the best terms, even if they never slept together again. Now, days later, she still burned from the feel of his hands on her flesh, and she wasn't even upset that he hadn't texted again since the morning after.

"Esme, did you hear about the position opening up?"

She looked up at Natalie, hoping she didn't see any residual lust there from her Friday romp.

"What position? Who's leaving?"

Natalie tilted her head toward Roberta, who sat working at her desk along the far wall.

"Roberta? I didn't think she was retirement age yet." Esme kept her voice pitched low.

"There's a rumor that she has an illness and needs surgery," Natalie said.

"I hope it isn't cancer."

"Nobody knows. I heard from Allison yesterday, who was accidentally cc'd into an email going out to other branches of People's Credit Union, opening the position to new transfers."

While Esme felt a weight on her chest at the thought of the dear older woman leaving. At the same time, she couldn't stop the leap of excitement she felt at a new opportunity.

"What are the job requirements to apply?" she asked Natalie.

Her friend's eyes sprang wider. "Are you considering the job?"

"I'd love to have a chance. But I didn't finish college, and these days every employer wants a four-year degree no matter what it's in."

"You're right, but I would still ask Jason if you're interested."

"I will." She sent a look at his closed door. Since Zayden had confided in her that day about why he was looking to get a loan, she couldn't help but wonder about the status of it. When would he be in to follow up on the loan application? Her reasons were somewhat selfish—she wanted to see him again. But she truly hoped he succeeded with his ranch too.

After hearing some rumors about his childhood, she felt he deserved to find happiness.

Natalie moved off to her station again, and Esme closed her drawer and shut down her system. Another glance at Jason's door showed him moving around behind the glass. Before he left for the evening, she wanted to catch him.

After bustling through the lobby, she knocked on his door. He looked up from stacking paperwork into neater piles than they already were.

"Come in," he said, and she opened the door.

When he dropped his gaze directly to her breasts, she felt that familiar burn of irritation. The man was definitely a titty-talker. When she'd dubbed him that to Natalie, the woman burst out laughing, and the moniker stuck, since Jason couldn't seem to remember a woman had eyes and not just two lumps on her chest to speak to.

"Esme. What's up?" He finally met her gaze.

"I wondered if you have a moment to talk about the position that's coming open."

He stared at her for a second, long enough that she feared she'd overstepped. It wasn't public knowledge in this branch of the credit union, after all.

"Rumors fly fast, don't they? Did Roberta tell you she put in her resignation?"

She shook her head. "I know little about it, other than a position is coming open. I'd like to apply."

He glanced over her dress, blazer and heels. "Sit down." He circled his desk to his chair and scooted forward to rest his elbows on the desk. He wasn't bad looking in a buttoned-up way, but he was too chauvinistic for her taste.

Besides, she liked her men big. And fantastic in bed. Sure, her type had totally changed since meeting Zayden, but she believed she'd made a huge upgrade from Owen.

"You're interested in becoming the loan officer?" Jason asked, interrupting her thoughts that returned to Zayden far too often lately.

She nodded and folded her hands in her lap. "I don't want to be a teller forever. I'm grateful for the job, but I'd like to be open to opportunities."

"Yes, that's admirable. Let me read the job requirements to you."

She waited while he pulled up a screen on his computer. When he began to list the job duties and functions of the loan officer, she simply nodded. She knew all this from Roberta and Jason himself, who often did loans as well, which was the case with Zayden.

When he stated the skills necessary for the position, she ticked them off one by one in her mind. Some she was familiar with and some not so much, but she could learn.

He looked up at her. "One of the job requirements is a four-year college degree."

Her hopes plummeted. "It's a requirement?"

"It is preferred. We like a solid background in business and finance."

"I see."

"I believe you joined our team with an incomplete college degree?"

She hated that her face burned. Not only did she regret not finishing, giving up her studies to follow that idiot here to Stokes, she saw judgment on Jason's face.

"That's right," she said quietly.

He sat back in his chair, eyes roaming over her body and lingering too long on her crossed legs. She was about to thank him and walk out, when he spoke.

"I think you definitely have a chance at becoming the next loan officer here, Esme."

She blinked at him in surprise.

"You would require some... tutelage, of course."

"I would expect job training."

"I was thinking more along the lines of bringing you up to speed myself with some personal training."

Her stomach hollowed out. What was he saying?

"After lunch breaks, the other tellers are more than able to handle the slower times, and you could spend those hours with me." He dipped his gaze to her breasts again. "Learning the ropes."

A dread fluttered in the base of her stomach. By ropes did he mean the job? Because that gleam in Jason's eye said otherwise.

Still, he was her boss, a professional, and he wouldn't risk his career by hitting on her, would he? No, he was far too intelligent for that. She must be reading more into things due to her perception of the man.

"That is very generous of you, Jason. I appreciate you taking the time to speak with me about this, and your offer is one I will consider."

He nodded. "We have some time. If you want to talk about it after hours, here's my personal number." He wrote it on the back of his business card and pushed it across the desk to her.

Her mouth dried out, but she took the card, unknowing what else to do right this minute.

"Take the night to think on it."

Was it her imagination, or had he stressed the word *night*?

"I will. Thank you." She stood, aware of his stare on her breasts once more. Twisting for the door, she gave him a small smile, all she could muster. Suddenly, the idea that she had a fighting chance at the promotion didn't seem so exciting.

When she walked back through the lobby to go to the breakroom and gathered her belongings to leave for the day, Natalie hurried over.

"How'd it go?"

She didn't know how to respond. On the surface, Jason was providing her an opportunity despite her shortcomings in the requirements. But she didn't feel good about the knot left in her stomach from the meeting.

"I'm going to think about it overnight."

"He offered you the job?"

"No. He offered me some training to bring me up to speed."

"That's great!" Natalie's smile grew wide, but she didn't feel much like smiling back.

"Thanks. We'll see. Like I said, I'm going to think on things." She slipped on her winter coat and changed out of her high heels into sensible boots to walk across the icy parking lot to her car.

"See you tomorrow." Natalie threw her a wave as she left.

"Have a good night," she responded.

The trip home didn't take long enough to offer time to think. In her house, she bumped up the thermostat a notch and changed into comfortable clothes. When she wandered into the kitchen to see what she could prepare for dinner, she started to evaluate her life. Picking it apart bit by bit, she started to wonder if a life change might be in order.

None of her family lived in Stokes. She could move back home to Tennessee and find another job.

But she'd grown to love the small, quaint town. She even enjoyed her job at the credit union and the people she worked with—besides, Jason.

In addition to the wording of his offer—and her questions about what he really was asking of her—she'd be working more directly with him if she got this new position. Could she handle that, for a couple more bucks per hour and a desk of her own?

With a sigh, she pulled out a pot and filled it with water. After setting it to boil on the stove, she located some pasta, canned clams and sauce. It wasn't the most gourmet dinner, but she was a mediocre cook and this would satisfy her hunger.

Maybe she could use some company. If she called Zayden, would he come over?

Days ago, she'd told him it was just sex, but now she realized it was more than sleeping with a hot guy that she needed. She needed friendship…and someone to be there for her.

What the heck—she'd give him a call. It was a day of steps forward. Nothing to lose but pride, but she'd survived that before, right?

Her heart did a hard belly-flop as she dialed his number. When he answered, he sounded a bit out of breath.

"It's me."

"Hey, sweetheart."

His drawled endearment set her heart bucking like a bull. She imagined it thrashing around her chest for eight full seconds before she could think what to say to him.

"You sound like you're working. Am I interrupting?"

"Yup." A smile seeped into his tone. "But I wouldn't answer if I didn't want to."

The man was as straightforward as they came, which helped when she was known for falling for false promises. With Zayden, what she saw was what she got. She wanted sex? She got the hottest night of her life and four orgasms. She needed someone to rescue her off the side of a mountain? Zayden showed up on his white horse.

"Hey, have you figured out your horse's name yet?"

"My horse... yeah, I call it Zeus."

"A majestic name for a beautiful beast." She wasn't thinking of the horse, but of the rider. Her stomach quivered with longing.

"I thought so too. So what's up, Esme? You stranded somewhere after another bad date?"

She chuckled. "No. I just got off work and I'm making dinner."

"What's on the menu?"

You, if you'll come over.

"Linguini with clam sauce."

"Clams?"

"Yeah. Nothing fancy — they're out of a can."

"Everything's fancier with you, Esme."

Her mouth fell open. It took her a heartbeat to find a snappy reply to override the mushy feelings coursing through her. "Kissing up doesn't get you a better meal."

He laughed, a hearty sound that heated her from the toes up. "Too bad. I could go for a steak."

Some might find his bad manners irritating, but she thought he was funny. "Better head to the steakhouse then."

"I want to come over. Is this an invitation or not?"

"For dinner, yes."

"All right. And Esme...we'll negotiate dessert when I get there." The grit in his voice was pure insinuation.

Breath nonexistent in her lungs, she floundered for a response to his teasing. She couldn't lie and say she wasn't loving it. The cowboy was definitely mixing it up for her.

"How soon can you be here?" she asked.

"Give me a few to finish up here and change clothes, then I'll be over. Will the linguini hold?"

"Yes. I'm switching off the boiling pasta water now. I'll prepare it in a bit. Talk to you soon." She ended the call and leaned against the counter, grinning and replaying their talk in her mind.

Conversation with the man always entertained, that was certain. There were no trivial discussions — he got straight to the point, even if it stung to hear like her past boyfriend issues.

But she was keyed up and couldn't deny the excitement bouncing around her insides at the thought of seeing him again.

She glanced down at her attire of leggings and an oversized sweatshirt. Not exactly sexy, but she'd vowed not to try too hard after that lacy teddy incident in the mountain cabin. She was finished putting on façades, and Zayden never bothered to.

She did, however, go into the bathroom to try to tame her curls and spritz herself with body spray.

Waiting was the hard part. Briefly again, she considered meeting him at the door wearing nothing but her bra and panties.

No, she was determined to be herself and not some parody of sexiness she believed guys wanted. She'd come to realize they didn't respect that. They got their jollies off and then walked away anyhow.

She and Zayden started as friends, then become friends who screwed. That seemed like as good a place to start as any. And friends didn't answer the door in thong underwear.

After giving him what she hoped was a good amount of time to finish his chores and get on the road, she started the water boiling again for pasta. As she cooked, she hummed to music she turned on her phone and tried to steer her thoughts into a calm direction.

Just because she was seeing Zayden didn't mean anything would happen between them. He might just kiss her between the eyes like he had after dancing together that night.

Which Zayden would she be getting? The man who held back from her or the one who swept her off her feet and carried her to bed with dark promises in his eyes?

While she liked both, a lot, tonight she hoped blowing off steam meant rolling naked in her sheets.

* * * * *

He'd seen Esme in the worst moments of her life and in the throes of ecstasy. She'd been dolled up for dates and even in work clothes. But he'd never seen her dressed down and comfortable, and the effect blew him away.

As she moved from stove to cupboard for a big bowl to dump the pasta dish into, he latched his gaze onto her every move. That loose sweatshirt hid all her assets, but the fact that he knew everything hiding under that thick cotton made him throb with desire.

Over the weekend, he'd found himself reliving their night together more than once. Hell, he'd been hard half a dozen times just from those memories, and now he was aching again.

His cock stretched the fly of his jeans. He made no move to cover his arousal. He wanted her, pure and simple.

When she moved to the sink, the fabric of her sweatshirt molded to her front, outlining her body. His balls clenched, and he nearly growled.

Turning to him, she served up a smile with a side of pasta. "Want to grab those plates and silverware for me while I carry this to the table?" She held his gaze for a thudding heartbeat.

Yeah, there was more going on between the two of them than he wanted to admit. Attraction wasn't new to him, but intrigue was. He didn't normally want to see a woman more than one time, and after he got what he wanted, he hit the road. But last time, some emotion had tugged at him to stay in bed with her, to tuck her against him and feel her curls tickling his chest.

Leaving her that night had twisted him up good. But in the end, he'd forced himself to go. It was best for both of them.

For it being best, I sure jumped at seeing her tonight.

She set the bowl on the table and shot him a glance. He picked up the plates and silverware and carried them to the table for two.

As she sat down, he seated himself across from her, and their gazes met. "I hope you're hungry," she said softly.

He was starving—for her.

"I've never had clam sauce, so I'm curious."

She used a serving spoon and placed a pile of pasta on his plate. It smelled good, and his empty stomach growled. Suddenly, he remembered his hat and removed it, setting it to the side.

She eyed him as she dumped a smaller portion on her own dish. "I hope you like it. If you don't, we can order a pizza or something."

"It's fine. You don't have to accommodate me, you know. Or is that your way with guys?"

She sucked in a sharp breath, pausing with her fork dug into the noodles. "I shouldn't be shocked that you say what you're thinking."

"Well, do you? Kiss up to men?" He took a bite and chewed. Flavors mingled on his tongue, something unusual but delicious.

After a long minute, she took a bite too. When she swallowed, she said, "I think that's part of my trouble with guys. But I'm changing my ways."

"Good."

She leveled that steady green stare on him. What he saw there... Hell, she burned for him.

160

A long second passed, then another.

What was he waiting for? She gave him fuck-me eyes and he couldn't be harder.

He dropped his fork with a clatter. He shoved to his feet, and she did too. Across the small table and an uneaten supper, they faced each other.

He clenched his hands at his sides. "I should hold back."

"Hold back from what?" Her voice came out whispery.

"From picking you up and carrying you to bed. From stripping off that sweatshirt that's driving me wild to see your curves underneath. And then from licking every inch of you from your neck to your little pinky toe."

Her chest rose and fell with quick breaths. "Why is doing that a bad thing?"

"Because—" he swallowed hard, "—having you in my arms again is the worst idea I've had in a while."

She stepped around the table and stopped inches away from him. With her head tipped back, her curls fell in a cloud. "Let me take the decision off your shoulders then."

She moved in. Circling his neck with her arms, she pulled him down for a kiss. The second their lips brushed, she issued a moan that yanked a deep growl from him. No choice left, he pulled her flush against him.

Her body molded to his in all the right ways. Too right.

Goddammit, he didn't know how to do relationships. Closest he'd come to interacting with a person normally was with Mimi.

Skating a hand down Esme's waist to land on her hip, he angled his head and teased her lips apart. She opened to him, and he didn't immediately plunge inside or take charge. Teasing her parted lips with his tongue, he brought her onto tiptoe.

Soft puffs of air escaped her. Lord, her sounds had been tormenting him for days.

That sharp intake of breath when he entered her.

The low moans that told him she hovered close to blinding release.

And then the throaty cries that came after. Hell, even her soft sigh as she made a pillow out of his chest had haunted his every waking—and sleeping—minute.

Pulling back, she looked into his eyes. Hers glittered with wanting. How could he deny her?

"Take me to bed, cowboy."

She didn't need to ask twice. He picked her up, and she twined her legs around his waist. The thin cotton leggings she wore were no barrier against the burning heat coming from her pussy, and his cock gave a hard jerk.

He knew her house, had spent hours in her bed. He didn't waste time laying her down on the mattress or capturing her lips in a tongue-tangling kiss.

How much teasing could she endure? He'd find out.

When he dragged that sweatshirt over her head, the sight of her full curves struck him again. Esme wasn't stick-thin like some, and he liked a little more weight on his women — not that he'd ever had any to call his. He could have had plenty. One even tried to snag him with a false pregnancy. Those had been the worst two weeks of his life, before he'd learned the truth and walked away.

This woman, though... He could come back for more again and again.

She gripped at his shoulders. He teased a fingertip down the crest of her breast to the point, up over the ridge and down the other side, before he followed the path over her bra with his lips. The silk and lace was warm from her skin. He closed his eyes, savoring her scents and the feel of her rising and falling under his caress.

Glancing up into her stare was a bad mistake. Her eyes glowed, and damn if he didn't want to see that more often. A heady power came over him.

He lifted his head and moved to her other breast. This time he bit down on her straining nipple, dragging a cry from her.

"Suck it, Zayden. I need your mouth on me. Please." She cupped his nape, guiding him.

Jesus, he wouldn't last long if they continued this way, and he didn't only mean orgasms and control. If he had her two more times... Hell, he already felt himself slipping.

He didn't do relationships. This wasn't him.

But was it the man he was meant to be?

* * * * *

A ragged breath escaped Esme's lips, and she squeezed her eyes against the scorching burn inside her. She needed it to end — wanted it to last.

Zayden had her stripped bare, and his rough fingers worked her into a fever. When he nudged her thighs apart, she looked down to watch the sexiest man alive about to feast on her soaking pussy.

He rumbled a groan against her flesh, and she bucked upward in response. He continued to take his slow time, pressing kisses over her mound of trim pubic hair, bypassing her neediest spot to spatter more kisses down her inner thighs. He licked a trail back up, and she shuddered as his hot breath washed over her slick folds.

She twisted her fingers in the longer locks on his nape. "I need you."

"That so?" he drawled, gaze intense on hers.

"Please."

"You want this?" He darted his tongue over her clit, lifting a thousand nerve endings to his touch.

She bucked. "Yes!"

"And this?" Thumbing apart her outer lips, he ran the point of his tongue through her wet folds to her core. When he dipped inside, her heart thudded to a stop, and she quit breathing too.

With her head thrown back, she could only nod for more.

Issuing a growl, he slid his hands under her ass, lifted her, and dived in. She lost sight of the universe. It drew to a faraway pinprick of light in the black bliss of her mind. Each rotation of his tongue around her clit, every nibble made her tip further into the throes of ecstasy.

When he lowered her to the mattress, she opened her eyes to find his gaze fixed on her. A shock of something more hit her... Something too overwhelming to name right now.

Then he reached between her legs and thrust two fingers inside her.

As her body clamped down on his callused digits, she couldn't look away. While he eased his fingers free of her body, their gazes held. Each time he plunged inside again, their stares locked in place.

Did he feel this insane drive to get closer like her? She was probably being stupid. Men didn't think that way. She had to take this for what it was—insanely hot, mind-blowing sex.

She curled her toes into the sheets and rocked in time to his tongue and fingers. As he rubbed over the perfect point deep in her pussy, she tightened.

An animalistic noise rumbled through him. He pressed his fingertips downward, and she burst with a wild cry.

Chapter Nine

"Fucking hell, why am I always still dressed when all I want is to drive my cock into you?" He tore at his clothes, not removing his stare from the woman still twitching on the bed from her release.

Her eyes appeared heavy with lust, her body flushed. He couldn't get out of his boots and jeans fast enough. Even as he shoved off his boxer briefs, he had a condom in the other hand, rolling it over the tip of his erection.

The thick shaft in his hand felt overly sensitive, his arousal at a twelve out of ten. It didn't help that she licked her lips at the sight of it.

He settled the condom at the base and pumped his cock once, thighs steel-hard as he moved forward. When he hovered over her, he entangled their fingers and stretched her arms overhead. Pinned, she only spread her legs for him.

With a shudder of need, he poised at her center.

"I've never wanted anybody the way I want you," she whispered.

There it was again—that burning in his chest like it had swollen ten times its size and been scourged in flames at the same time. She made him feel more than good, and he didn't want to think about why.

She lit up his insides, which had been darkened his entire life.

Tightening her hold on his hands, she wet her lips. "Take me, Zayden."

"Nothing could stop me, sweetheart."

He drove in. The minute her slippery hot walls enveloped his cock, he slammed his mouth over hers. Their passion raged on through lips, teeth and tongues. She dragged her mouth free and bit into his neck. He churned his hips faster. The moment was getting away from him. It was coming too fast, too soon, too…

He stole a look at her face, only to find her focused on him, eyes full of passion, lip trapped in her teeth.

Letting go was like water flowing over a cliff. Like galloping on a good horse.

When he exploded, he bit down on a roar, but it didn't stop the sound from echoing. She got her hands free of his clasp and wrapped her arms around him, riding out the storm of a release so huge that he couldn't form a coherent thought.

"Sweetheart… Jesus."

She pressed a kiss to his jaw, and then landed one on his lips that had him moaning out. The need to keep going was so strong. He rolled her atop him, and she flashed a heart-stopping grin.

When his heart picked up the beat again, he cupped her breasts and watched several emotions flicker across her face.

Flattening a hand to her spine, he drew her down on him, slowly. The soft, damp curves of her body and her weight on him felt good. He didn't want to get up for a long time.

Maybe the moment had come to examine the changes in his life. Not only had he decided something he never thought he would — to stay on at the ranch he'd vowed never to return to — but he lay here with a woman he didn't want to let go.

She stroked a hand up his side, shifting into a more comfortable position draped over him. "Am I squashing you?"

He chuckled. "Far from it. I was thinking how good you feel." The admission took some doing. He wasn't a man who expressed much. Through the years, anger remained his most reliable friend. Right now, the emotion was completely absent in him...and it was shocking as hell.

At this moment, he couldn't give a crap about how his father had fucked him up or he'd fucked up his own life. He didn't care that his mother didn't love him and his brothers enough to take them with her when she left. For the first time in forever — maybe ever — he had peace.

As minutes passed, their breathing slowed. In the other room a clock ticked, the fridge hummed, and a faucet dripped.

"You've got a leaky faucet," he said.

"I know. I haven't gotten around to calling the landlord. Zayden?"

He tensed, prepared for something he wasn't ready to hear. "What is it?"

"I liked dessert."

A grin spread over his face and then through his soul. He hugged her closer. "I didn't even give you the ice cream on top."

She pushed away, palms on his chest, looking down at his face. "You're holding out on me? There's better sex to be had?"

He arched a brow and gave her a lazy smile. "Try me."

"I like a challenge."

"So do I." With a jolt, he realized it was true. He'd often taken the lazy route — get it done and move on. But with Esme, that wasn't the case, and he wanted to show her just how she should be treated, even if only for a short while.

In the ocean, waves didn't last. One always disappeared as another swelled in the distance, Mimi always said. All things came to an end, and this would be no different...

But he was living for the present.

He jumped up and tossed her over his shoulder, making his way to the shower with her squeals of delight ringing like bells.

* * * * *

Soaping each other up and rinsing each other off gave her more of a thrill than it should. She could spend a lot of time studying the chiseled muscle of Zayden's body. The man embodied a six-foot-tall work of art.

Water sluiced over his tanned back and over his muscled ass. Just looking at the man made her burn with want.

When she dug her thumbs lightly into his shoulders, he leaned against the shower wall and moaned. She continued to knead the knotted muscles till she felt them relax.

"What do you do on the ranch to get so sore?" she asked over the rush of water.

"Right now, I'm trying to fix things. A lot has gone untended for too long and if I'm staying, I have to repair it. Trouble is, I don't have much to work with and funds are short."

"No word from the credit union on that loan yet?" She thought of Jason's offer concerning the job opening, and her insides coiled with disgust. She had a very bad feeling about the man. Recently, she'd learned she needed to rethink her opinions of people and see them for what they were. Her ex led her on and she'd moved to Stokes on his promise that their love would last forever. Then Owen led her up the mountainside, and look how that had turned out.

171

At least Zayden hadn't made any promises, and she was glad of it. Even if her heart went crazy just from being close to the man, she wouldn't commit to more than what they had going right this minute.

"No calls yet," he said. "Mimi would have told me."

Her brows crinkled, and she stopped massaging his shoulders. "Who's Mimi?"

"Closest I've ever had to a momma or grandma, I guess you could say. She came to live with us when I was a teen, and she never left. She takes care of things around the house."

"I see. Was she involved with your... father?"

He tensed, and she feared her questioning hit a different kind of sore spot.

Tossing her a look, he rinsed off again. "Not that I ever knew of. She isn't that dumb."

She chewed her lip. "I'm sorry for asking. I've heard..." She stopped, sticking her foot in it even deeper.

"What have you heard?" Before she could answer, he went on. "That I'm a no-good Moon? That my father was a deadbeat drunk who knocked his kids around, and my brothers and I are cut from the same cloth?"

"I-I...hadn't heard that, no."

He made a sharp movement and switched off the shower, leaving her standing there cold and wet and shut out.

He took a long look at her and then his face softened. After grabbing a fluffy towel, he opened it and wrapped it around her, lifting her out of the shower and setting her on the bathmat.

"I'm sorry," he said gruffly, reaching for a second towel to rub her hair with. Her curls would be a frizzy afro when he was finished, and it would take her ages to right them before she could leave the house again, but she didn't protest his ministrations.

Head bent, he slowed his touch, working the towel over her scalp and down her shoulders. Silence built between them.

She reached up and stilled his hand, drawing the towel off her head. "Zayden, I don't listen to rumors, and they aren't something I believe anyway. I know very well how rumors can get blown out of proportion. Have you heard the one about Owen and I getting into a fight and how he threatened to throw me off the mountain?"

He met her gaze. "No." A tendon in his jaw leaped. "But if he had, I would have hunted him down, Esme."

A shiver ran through her. He sounded serious, his tone rough. And if she knew anything about Zayden Moon's character, it was that he was dead set on any statement he made. If he told her he could break Owen's legs, he could. If he claimed he could pleasure her better than any other man on earth, well, her body still hummed from that promise kept.

She pulled another towel off the shelf and began rubbing the water off his broad shoulders and chest. When she hit his abs, she noted he was growing hard.

"Maybe it's time for more dessert," she said softly.

Throwing him a teasing smile, she dropped to her knees and took him in her mouth.

* * * * *

Zayden groaned as he realized he was, for the third time in an hour, reliving the memory of Esme's tongue riding the ridge of his swollen cock. Then her licking down the shaft with scorching flicks of her tongue, and finally encompassing his balls in liquid heat.

Each time his cock bumped at the back of her throat, he groaned louder, until the need to take over grew too strong to ignore. He'd fisted his hands in her hair and dragged her lips down over his erection till the hip-churning end.

Christ, he had to get a grip on this infatuation.

The wrench he used to torque the engine part slipped, and his knuckles bashed against steel.

"Motherfucking hell," he bit out, shaking his hand and glaring at the tractor. Who was he kidding? It was dead, and no amount of elbow grease would revive it. His father hadn't bothered to start it all these years, and now the engine was frozen up, useless.

174

He turned his face up to the sky and sent his father a curse, wherever he was. "Screw you, Dad!"

Bending to swipe the wrench off the ground, he drew three calming breaths and started over. Once he set his mind to a task, he didn't give up easy, and he was going to do his best to get this tractor up and running. He needed it to put his plan into action — get the back pasture cleared and ready for hay.

His mind trundled ahead, over more plans. Secure that loan. If the credit union wouldn't consider loaning him the money, he'd find another bank. Too bad the rancher's coalition was finished with the Moons, or he'd ask them too.

He got a good, tight hold on the part he wanted to loosen and used his strength.

The wrench didn't slip this time — but the part busted clean off.

Zayden stepped back, fury rushing over him. For a heartbeat, he considered throwing himself at the tractor and sinking his fists into the steel side, but all that would do was put him out of commission with a broken hand. Besides, punching the tractor wouldn't help, when really he wanted to beat the shit out of his father.

Yeah, rage was good, and he could use that to make things happen. He was just turning away from the dead hunk of steel to head into the house and call the credit union, when he saw the SUV round the bend in the drive. He stood watching the vehicle approach, and soon could read the letters on the side.

175

Son of a bitch. The sheriff.

That couldn't be good. At all.

His mind darted to the crumpled fine on the floor of his truck and the community service he hadn't bothered to set up.

Yanking a hanky from his back pocket, he wiped the motor oil from his hands and walked toward the sheriff.

The man settled his hat more firmly against the Colorado mountain breeze and looked to Zayden. "Howdy, Moon."

"Sheriff." The man didn't look familiar.

He sauntered up, looking around. "Haven't been up here in a while."

Zayden leveled a stare at him. "What's this about?"

He waited to hear more about his run-in with Deputy Dickies. The sheriff turned to gaze toward the pasture where the few horses were grazing.

"How many horses you got here on the Moon Ranch?" he asked.

"Five."

"You sold some recently."

Zayden narrowed his eyes. "I sold one to the neighbor."

"What happened to the other five?"

Arching a brow, Zayden tried to tamp down the rage rising inside him. "When I got here, there were

176

only six horses on the ranch, and a handful of cattle out in the west pasture. What's going on?"

"Was about to ask you the same thing." The sheriff squared his shoulders and faced Zayden. "Your father stole those horses."

Zayden's chest burned. "I don't know a thing about it, but if you'd like to question him, he's up in the Stokes Cemetery."

"I heard. The bastard died before we could connect him with the crime."

"Yeah, he was always a son of a bitch, but I can't help ya."

"Mind if I have a look at your horses?"

For a long moment, he didn't respond. But what good would it do to deny the sheriff? He'd just return with a search warrant.

He nodded and turned for the field. The sheriff followed.

"How did you make this discovery?" he asked the lawman.

"About four months back, we got a call that six horses had been stolen out of a pasture in the middle of the night."

He shook his head. "Couldn't be my father."

"Why do you say that?"

"Because he was drunk off his ass every night of his life. There's no way he'd be able to stand on his own two feet, let alone steal off with six horses."

"The rancher had a trail camera up to see if he could find out what was killing his chickens, and your father was caught on tape."

Well, that was new. The old man was remotely sober after noon?

Zayden didn't have anything to add to the conversation as he led the sheriff to the pasture. When they stopped at the fence, the man pulled out his cell phone and held it up to compare photos of the stolen horses on the screen to those cropping hay in Zayden's field.

"None of 'em are branded, Sheriff."

"That's because they'd just been purchased at auction and the owner hadn't gotten around to it yet."

When he held up the phone, Zayden bit back a curse. Sure enough, the paint mare standing in his pasture matched the one on the screen, spot for spot.

"Looks like we found one."

He grunted but said nothing. What was there to say? He wasn't about to cover for the old man—he never had. He just fixed the shit his father wrecked in life, and even in death the asshole was screwing him over.

"The rest don't match," he told the sheriff after he flipped through the rest of the images. "Come back for the paint and leave me out of it."

"Mind if I have a look around?" The sheriff eyed him.

"All you'll find is a dead tractor and a lot of rundown buildings, Sheriff. Those horses right there are all I got on the property. If you want to go searching for more, then you show me a warrant first."

A long look passed between them, and Zayden stood his ground. It wasn't his first run-in with a lawman and it sure wouldn't be the last.

But dammit, when would it stop?

It can only stop with me.

The realization wasn't one he could face right now, but he sure would be thinking hard on it later.

"I got work to do. You can see yourself out." He waved toward the driveway.

The sheriff gave a short nod and walked away.

When he'd gotten into his SUV and driven off, Zayden tore off his hat and pinched the bridge of his nose hard. At least it wasn't the white horse, but the paint was the next best in the herd, and since it was still young, he'd considered training it. The animal would have fetched a decent price, but now that couldn't happen.

He walked into the house. Mimi sat at the sewing machine, doing some of her side work. The thin wisps of white hair falling on her shoulders gave him a pang to see how she'd aged. When had it happened?

Living with his father, it was a wonder she'd kept any hair at all. If he'd continued to live with him, he would have pulled out every last strand on his head.

179

"Mimi."

She didn't move, just kept sewing.

He said her name two more times, and still she didn't hear him. When he touched her shoulder, she turned, and he saw that it wasn't the sewing machine that she couldn't hear over — the woman had earbuds in and was listening to music.

Zayden's chuckle took him by surprise. "What are you listening to?"

"Luke Bryan. He's real good."

He bobbed his head. "That he is."

"What did you need, Zayden?"

"Sheriff's comin' up to get the paint in the pasture."

Her eyes flew open wide and then redness seeped into her cheeks. The Indian coloring didn't conceal the fact she was blushing.

Zayden stared at her. "You knew."

She compressed her lips, making lines pop out around them. "I guessed when new horses showed up here on the ranch. I couldn't think where your father would get enough money for horses, but I wondered if he'd won them in a bet."

Great. He was into gambling in the final years too.

"Well, one of them's stolen property. Hell, all of them might be."

They stared at each other and he sighed. "Not your responsibility, Mimi. I'll handle it. I just wanted to tell you I'm going to ride out to the herd and the sheriff will be coming."

She nodded, stuffed the earbud back into her ear and returned to her sewing.

When he walked back out of the house, he swore at the situation, but no words could make things better. He was chained to a sinking ship, with stolen cargo and no way to stay afloat.

No, he wasn't stuck. He could leave. Selling the property might be the only option, and Mimi had told him she could move to town and start over without the Moons dragging her down. The woman deserved a better life.

Didn't he?

He'd believed that by leaving Stokes he could find something different for himself, but now he realized he'd just continued to mess up. In Stokes or another town, location didn't matter when *he* was the reason for his life being at a dead end.

His thoughts returned to Esme. The woman deserved a good man, not the likes of him. He had to quit dicking around with her before he hurt her. The last thing he wanted was to be another mistake in her life.

She'd told him she was changing her ways. What did that mean? She wasn't going to date anymore? He guessed in a few years, she'd have a ring on her finger and a baby-on-board sticker on the back of her car.

The thought gave him a pang. Jealousy never mixed well with him, and he shoved the green snake away.

After saddling Zeus, he rode out. His mind clung to memories of Esme in this very saddle with him.

A better life began with him, with him making better choices and working hard.

He had everything he needed right here on the ranch—land to plant and feed the animals he put here. Even if he had to buy one horse at a time, he could fill the gaps with odd jobs in town. Esme would move on.

How often would he run into her? Would he be able to see her holding another man's hand?

Why couldn't he shake the woman from his brain? She hadn't only curled up in his arms—she'd found a way into his heart, and it would take a hell of a lot to evict her again, but he had to try.

He was a drunk's son. A thief's son. He didn't even have a high school diploma and nothing but a string of prior arrests behind him, a few bucks and some fallow land to his name now. He had to let her go.

When he crossed from Moon lands to Ute territory, he turned his horse toward the houses backed up against the lake. He hadn't been here in years, but he knew the layout well enough to locate Mimi's great-nephew.

The house had a brand-new green metal roof, and the white siding looked in good repair. Ouray must be doing well for himself. As he neared the house, Ouray appeared at the front door.

"Moon. Everything all right on the ranch?" His appearance reminded him of Mimi.

He dismounted and kept hold of the reins. "Good to see ya, Ouray. Been a long time."

The man faced him with a smile. "It has." They shook hands, and he was glad for his friendship and all he had done for the ranch—and his great-aunt. Zayden carried guilt over leaving her, but knowing she had her great-nephew at her back lessened the sting.

"I came with a few questions." Zayden didn't beat around the bush.

He nodded. "I'm listening."

"You wouldn't know anything about some horses that showed up on the ranch, 'bout four months back, would you?"

Ouray's dark eyes penetrated him. "I know they were sold."

"To whom? Ute?"

"Yes."

"Damn," he said quietly. Getting the horses back from someone on the reservation meant he'd need to come up with the funds to pay for them. It burned, knowing he would have to buy them back, only to turn them over to the sheriff. It was the right thing to do, but would he ever get ahead in life or escape the chaos his father left behind?

"How much? Do you know?" he asked Ouray.

"Three thousand apiece."

"Jesus," he drawled.

"They were good trail horses. The man who bought them uses them for trail rides for visitors. He makes back what he put in."

"Hell." How could he come up with fifteen grand? He wasn't digging his way out of this mess anytime soon, and the prospect of walking away from it all and giving it the middle finger on the way out the door looked better and better.

"I have to buy them back," he said.

Ouray raised a brow. "It's a lot of money."

"I'll get it. Can you tell me where this man lives?"

He pointed. "Over the rise, follow the road. You can't miss the ranch or the sign for trail rides."

Zayden bowed his head. "Thank you." He gathered the reins in his hand, prepared to swing back into the saddle and head home again. Pausing, he turned to Ouray. "Thank you for all you've done for me on the ranch. And for your great-aunt."

"Chipeta is an elder, and we take care of our family." His simple statement left Zayden with a hollow ache in his chest for something he'd never have—a family way of life he'd never experience.

Nodding, he put his foot in the stirrup and hitched his leg over the horse. When he guided it back home, he took the route past the ranch where the horses were.

Damn his father to hell. No—make that the seventh circle of hell. He deserved to burn for all this underhanded mess he'd created and then saddled Zayden with. If his brothers were here, together they might figure out a way to rally the funds to buy back the stock, but alone? There weren't enough trees in all of Stokes to cut down that would pay for this fucked-up crime.

All the way home, he brooded over the facts. He came up with answers and then discarded them. By the time he reached the ranch lands again, the only thing he knew for certain was his dad was lucky he was dead, because otherwise, Zayden would strangle him with his bare hands.

As soon as he returned from his ride, he found a message waiting for him, a voicemail left on his phone.

A seed of pain grew in his chest as he spotted her number... Esme. The last thing she needed was to get caught up in this with him. Best thing to do was ignore her, just delete the message without finding out what she wanted.

What if she really needs me, though?

With the phone clutched tight in his hand, he stared into space. Right this second, she could be in trouble.

Goddammit.

He brought the phone to his ear and listened. Her voice flooded him with wanting. His chest burned, and his cock twitched at the sweet tones in his ear.

Hi, Zayden. I'm on my lunch break, and well... I just wanted to hear a friendly voice.

Nobody ever called him friendly. The woman must be crazy.

At least she wasn't abandoned along a back road by some ex of hers or put into danger by a blind date. She only wanted to chat — with him.

I'm on break for another twenty minutes if you get this and want to call me back. Her flirty tone brought a smile to his lips.

I work 'til four o'clock and I'll be home around four-thirty. If you aren't busy... Don't feel obligated to call back. I was just thinking of you. Bye.

He checked the time on his phone against the time the voicemail was left. He'd missed her break time. He issued a long sigh and closed his eyes as her message ended.

Calling her back was a bad idea. Hadn't he already decided against seeing her?

Dammit. He wanted to hear her sweet voice again — she was the only good thing he'd found in Stokes or anywhere else, for that matter.

He swallowed hard. He was getting in too deep.

A voice spoke up in the back of his mind: *Sure you aren't already?*

Chapter Ten

Beer bottles clinked together as the waitress cleared off the table. "There ya go," she sang out, throwing Zayden a smile before she moved away.

He waved for Esme to sit. She sank to the wooden chair and eyed the cowboy who seated himself across from her. A crinkle of strain between his brows had her wondering what put it there.

"I didn't think you would call me back," she said.

He rubbed his brow. "I wanted to see you."

He sounded less than enthusiastic about it. Maybe she should have stayed home instead of agreeing for him to pick her up and grab a pizza together.

"Bad day?" she asked.

He watched her direct her curls behind her ear, gaze heavy and full of too many questions for him to answer.

With a nod, he said, "You could say that."

Her day held some rough spots too. Jason called her into his office and asked again if she'd made a decision about spending a few hours a day with him, learning the ropes of the job opening. The way he looked at her and the innuendo in his tone were unmistakable.

Fact was, she decided almost from the start she wanted to refuse the offer, but she felt more than a little trapped. If she said no, could her job be at risk? She did want the promotion, just on her own terms.

She sighed. She needed to figure out a lot.

"Sounds like you've lived through a bad day too." Zayden gave her a hint of his crooked smile, the one that curled her toes and made her beg for his hands all over her.

"I don't really want to talk about it." She reached for the menu and flipped it open.

"Me neither." He did the same.

While he read the selection, she shot glances at him. He hadn't shaved in what looked like a day or two. The dark stubble coating his jaw made her thighs tingle. She clamped them together and tried to ignore the pangs of need shooting through her lower belly.

She wanted him—that was undeniable. But if she didn't want to lose her heart to the wrong man again, she had to figure out where his mind was in all this. Zayden was a lot of colors of the rainbow, vibrant and full of life. But mixed together, they would make gray. She needed to know where he stood with her.

Most men were different from women. They separated sex from emotions and didn't think much of the act as a bond between people. And while she wasn't prepared to jump into another relationship, being with Zayden made her feel way more warm and fuzzy than simple lust ever could.

She'd probably opened herself up to another letdown. But the look in his eyes told her she could be wrong.

He caught her gaze—their eyes clung. When he tore his stare away and riveted it on the menu, she tried to shuck off her breathlessness and focus on what to order.

"How hungry are you?" he asked.

She wet her lips. "Very."

His gaze shot to hers, and they shared a knowing smile. Her flirtatious reply was obviously going to lead them out the door and straight into each other's arms. The chemistry was off the charts, the attraction hotter and more dangerous than anything she'd experienced with other men. But she couldn't read Zayden Moon.

She leaned forward. "Pepperoni?"

His lips tipped upward in that sexy-as-sin quirk that made her knees weak. When the waitress walked back over, it was clear from the toss of her hair and wide smile she was affected by the cowboy as well.

Eyeing Esme, he said, "Pepperoni pizza and cheese sticks for an appetizer?"

Her gaze floated down to his hard mouth. Those lips could do so much damage to her body, shaking it apart with mind-blowing releases.

He noted the direction of her stare and smiled. The waitress shifted from foot to foot, probably just as affected by that smile. "Is that all for you two?"

Esme nodded, and the server moved off, leaving them alone again.

Silence fell between them, loaded with what felt like dynamite. One glance and they'd explode.

A shivery breath escaped her, and she toyed with her hair, pushing it off her face. When the curls bounced forward again, she twisted one around a forefinger while Zayden tracked the movement with lidded eyes.

"You know what you're doing to me, Esme."

"Same thing you're doing to me." She lifted a hand to her own cheek and rubbed a finger over it to indicate his growth of beard.

He sat back in his chair and avoided looking at her directly for a long minute. "How was work?"

"Well, I dealt with a very disgruntled customer today. The man screamed at me and told me that I was wrong, that his account wasn't overdrawn."

"Was it?"

She nodded.

"What do you do when people don't have enough to cover their debts?"

She shrugged. "Not much that I can do. I state the facts and the terms and conditions of the account. Often they ask to speak to the manager." At mention of the manager, her stomach gave a twist, like a small dagger digging deep into the flesh.

When she looked up, he watched her with intensity, a dark glimmer in his eyes. "What else happened?"

"Nothing."

"You're paler than you were a minute ago."

Am I? Who notices things like that anyway?

"Everything is fine. Boy, I'm hungry." The last thing she wanted to talk about was Jason and his offer.

Luckily, their cheese sticks arrived in a paper-covered basket, the scents heaven to her hungry stomach. She took a batter-dipped stick and pushed the basket toward Zayden. Just the sight of his long fingers pinching the food and drawing it to his lips had her squeezing her thighs again.

He watched her take a bite. He took one too. Then she swirled her tongue around her cheese stick, and he groaned.

"Esme…"

"Hmm?" She did it again, this time slipping the end between her lips. He watched her for a pounding heartbeat, and then she abruptly bit the end off.

His crooked grin was enough reward for her teasing. She smiled back, and some of the tension between them eased.

"Were you glad I called?" she asked.

"Actually, yeah. I needed a distraction."

She looked at him harder. "You know you can talk to me, right? We *are* friends, and I've told you loads about my life and problems."

He hesitated and swallowed the rest of his cheese stick. "It's complicated."

"What isn't in this world?"

"It's more complicated than most things."

"Well, I've been stranded on a mountain during a storm, so I'm pretty sure I can handle whatever it is you have to tell me." She nonchalantly plucked another cheese stick from the basket.

The weight of his sigh pressed down on her from across the table. She couldn't fathom what he was going through.

She searched his eyes. "What's going on, Zayden?"

"My father did something before he died. The sheriff paid me a visit today."

"Oh no." She'd heard a rumor at the credit union about some stolen horses. *Please don't let it be true. He's got enough to deal with.*

"Yeah, it's bad." He scrubbed a hand over his face. "I'll figure something out."

While he didn't tell her a single thing about the trouble in his lap, she felt compelled to ease him. Reaching across the table, she placed her hand over the back of his. He looked up into her eyes, and that shock of electricity hit again, harder this time. The sensation pinged up her arm and throughout the rest of her body, to land between her legs.

"You keep looking at me that way and we aren't waitin' on this pizza."

She tipped her head. "We could get it to go."

He pressed his lips together and looked away.

He held back from her. Even if he wanted her as badly as she did him—and she thought he did—he wouldn't make the first move. What stopped him?

When someone passed their table, Esme glanced up at her coworker Natalie. She was with a guy, and they were laughing. She spotted Esme and then took one look at Zayden and her jaw dropped.

Stopping before the table, she grinned in a way that had Esme cringing. If she lumped them together, it would have Zayden even more stiff and unbending to her attempts to get to know the man.

"So good to see you here," Natalie said to her.

"Hi, Natalie." She held out her hand toward Zayden, who sat like a statue. "This is Zayden Moon."

"I know who you are. You went to school with my sister."

He nodded but didn't ask who her sister was.

"Oh, this is Sam. We're meeting some friends to play pool. Want to join us?" She looked between them.

Zayden didn't move a muscle—not even a flicker of that muscle in the corner of his jaw that captivated Esme so often.

"Uh, we're waiting on our pizza, thanks. You guys have fun! I'll see you tomorrow at work."

Natalie rolled her eyes. "Ugh, don't remind me about work. Jason was in a bigger funk than usual today, don't you think? I kept thinking I was in trouble, the way he kept looking toward us tellers."

Esme dropped her gaze to the tabletop. "Yeah, he was in a bad mood." She knew it had everything to do with her, especially since his mood shifted after she told him she wasn't ready to commit to anything yet concerning the job.

"See you tomorrow." Natalie and her friend moved off, leaving them alone again.

The pizza arrived, and she couldn't find her appetite anymore.

"What's going on, Esme?"

Her gaze shot to Zayden's. "What do you mean?"

"I mean," he leaned across the table, big and hot as hell, "whenever someone brings up work or that boss of yours, you act weird."

"How do you know I'm acting weird? We don't know each other that well," she defended.

He cocked a brow. "Don't I know you?" He pitched his voice low. "I found a cold, wet and frightened woman half-frozen on a mountainside. I know how you feel when you're shaking with fear. I know how you feel in my arms, bare and with the taste of my seed on your lips."

She sucked in sharply.

His dark eyes pinned her gaze. "I know that you get tangled up with the wrong kind of men."

"Including you?" she said weakly, trying to get to the bottom of his mood swings concerning her.

"Including me," he growled out. "Especially me. But if there's something you need to tell me about this Jason guy, you'd better spill it, sweetheart."

She clenched her fingers together in her lap. "Why should I tell you when you won't tell me a single thing about the sheriff's visit and why it has you so upset?"

They shared an angry look, but sparks of something much more also flew between them, just like when they sat across her kitchen table. The air grew charged, and both of them remembered what had happened then.

Her breathing changed, and she dragged in an uneven breath. The waitress returned and asked if they wanted a box, and he waved a hand for her to go away. As usual with Zayden, the man was giving the middle finger to the world, even if the world had nothing to do with his anger.

He tossed a couple bills down on the table and stood.

"Let's go." His gritty tone had her clamping her thighs together again, but somehow she managed to stumble to her feet and reach for her belongings. On the way to the exit, Zayden reached back and grabbed her hand.

* * * * *

When the restaurant door swung shut behind them, he whirled Esme into his arms and backed her up against the side of the building. She tipped her face up to his, a come-screw-me look in her green eyes.

Hell, he shouldn't.

Could he stop it?

She got to him, in all ways, and not just physically. She was digging into his mind with her questions, her demands...and he was letting her. Dammit, he had to step back.

But her rosebud lips were a torment, and not one he could resist. He was weak—everyone in Stokes knew he'd always been weak.

Did he give a damn?

The puffy coat she wore created a thick barrier he didn't want between them. He needed to feel her curves pasted to his body while he drove his cock into her sweet, tight heat.

She hitched in a breath. "Zayden..."

"I can't." He pushed away and turned to go.

"You think you can walk away from me, but you can't, and we both know it." Anger infused her voice.

He stopped dead on the sidewalk. Without looking back, he said, "You're don't know what's between us any more than I do."

"Don't I? You keep trying to resist me, but here you are with me again, and this time it's not because I called for rescue. You keep coming to me because you want me, Zayden, and it isn't only sex."

He twisted to pierce her with his gaze. She was too fucking beautiful, and his heart cracked in two that he couldn't have her.

"You're wrong," he grated out.

"Come back over here, look me in the eyes and tell me I'm wrong. That you don't feel something for me besides lust. You can't stay away from me, but you've never had something like this before and you're afraid." She raised her chin a notch.

Goddammit, that expression of sheer conviction riled him. Who was she to say she knew what he was thinking, feeling? She didn't know jack about him.

Then why was he getting angrier as each word she spoke hit home?

The wind picked up her curls, causing them to riot around her face. With a quick flick of her fingers, she shoved them away. "You want to know about Jason?"

He waited.

Something in her eyes broke a little. "He propositioned me."

What the fuck? For a heartbeat, he stood on the rim of a volcano about to erupt.

Then fury hit him and it was too late to jump out of the way of the lava—he *was* the lava.

He strode back to her and grabbed her by the shoulders. "Why do you keep finding this kind of trouble with guys?"

"I didn't have anything to do with it. Not this time. I told you I was learning, making better decisions when it comes to men, and I have."

He didn't want to let her go, even as the urge to go find that asshole boss of hers and smash his teeth through his face blazed through him.

"There, I said it—you know what's been eating at me tonight. Now it's your turn." Those green eyes on his face shouldn't feel like the softest touch, but dammit, they did.

He glared down at her. All he wanted was a taste of her lips. "I'm not telling you about the sheriff."

"Then don't tell me. I want to hear you say that I'm wrong about us, that you don't feel something for me. Tell me, Zayden."

He tore his gaze away, and she bobbed her head to the side to capture it again. "Say it," she whispered, but her words were almost snatched by the wind. A storm was coming—he could smell the sharp tang of snow. And all he wanted was to be holed up with her somewhere quiet and alone, just the pair of them without a stitch of clothes between them.

He made a sound in his chest and released her.

She caught up with him at his truck and got in without even looking his way.

Since he'd picked her up, he had to drive her home. He'd be strong. He wouldn't let her get under his skin. Wouldn't put his hands on her.

Is that even possible?

* * * * *

He parked his truck in front of her house. At his side, Esme sat stiffly, scooted all the way against the door. Far from him.

She reached for the handle to jump out, and who could blame her for wanting to escape?

Catching her by the elbow, he swung her in the seat to look at him. When their gazes connected, he issued a sigh that sounded more like a growl.

"I'm an asshole." His statement dropped into the silence between them.

"Yes, you are."

"I deserve that. Hell, Esme...don't go like this." Oddly, she had become his one and only friend in the world. Maybe she understood more about him than he thought. She heard rumors, but she didn't toss it all in his face and call him a loser Moon like everyone else.

She shifted her stare from him and refused to look up again. Under his fingers, her arm tensed.

"I'm going inside," she said quietly.

He managed to unpeel his fingers from her and nodded.

She climbed out and slammed the door. He watched her take two steps up to the sidewalk. She didn't glance back at him.

He struck the steering wheel with the heel of his hand. "Dammit!"

In a blink, he was out of the truck and striding fast to close the distance between them. When she heard the thud of his boots on the sidewalk, she turned to look, and her jaw dropped.

"You deserve more than me, but I can't stay away from you...because there's more between us." He searched her eyes a split second before crushing his mouth over hers. A sound of wanting burst from her, and he pulled her against him. The wind tore at them, but neither of them seemed to notice as their lips collided with a need driven by animal attraction and fueled by anger.

She angled her head, and he plunged his tongue into her sweet, hot mouth.

"I fucking want you, sweetheart."

"I know you do." Her sassy response caught him off guard, and a laugh broke from his chest.

She twisted free of his hold and fumbled in her handbag for her house keys. When she pulled them out, he noted a slight tremor to her hand, and his heart ached to make it right with her.

He watched her put the key into the lock and twist it. She stepped out of the swirling snow and looked up at him.

"Can I come in?" A rough rasp filled his voice.

She stepped aside, and he entered, closing the door behind them. Silence fogged the space between them, and she gulped for air as he moved toward her.

Watching him, she dropped her bag to the floor. Her keys clattered.

He stared into her eyes. "I don't apologize often, but I'm sorry in advance for not being the man you think I am."

She unzipped her puffy coat and let it slide off her shoulders to the floor with the rest of her things. Circling his neck with her arms, she tipped her face up to his.

"You're the only one who doesn't believe in yourself." She brushed her lips across his with extreme gentleness he'd never known before. "I believe in you…"

"You're the only one. But it's enough." He yanked her flush against him, his hand under her curls, cradling her head in his palm.

Her lips bowed upward, and her smile sealed his fate. He brought her onto her toes and kissed her. Sweet torment blossomed in his core, but it was more than simple lust this time. Hell, if he was honest with himself, it hadn't just been lust those other times either. She'd burrowed into his heart that night on the mountain. She'd been in the arms of a complete stranger and hadn't questioned his past or motives at the time—all she'd done was allow him to keep her safe. Somehow, that was all he'd ever needed.

Breaking from the kiss, he stared down at her. "You trust me, don't you?"

"With my life. You know that."

A lump formed in his throat. "With your heart?"

Tears leaped into her eyes. "What are you asking of me, Zayden?"

Hell, he didn't know himself. Or maybe he did.

"That you take me for who I am."

She smoothed her fingers over his jaw, rasping his five o'clock shadow. "You idiot. I already do."

Her calling him an idiot brought another harsh laugh from him, but he gulped it back as he claimed her mouth again. He lifted her and turned for her bedroom.

When he set her on her feet, she pulled his head down and pressed a kiss to his neck. Then another. He groaned as she brushed her lips to his ear and nibbled the lobe. Burning up for her, he ran his hands down her torso, grazing the sides of her breasts as he did. The soft moan echoing from her lips had him as hard as stone.

With a grin, she plucked the hat from his head. She popped his shirt buttons one by one 'til she could ease her hands over his chest. At his belt, he stopped her.

Their gazes locked, and short pants made her breasts rise and fall.

He tried to tug the hem of her top free of her jeans, but it was stuck. She moaned out, and he looked at her in confusion.

"I'm wearing a bodysuit."

"What the hell's a bodysuit?"

"Like a swimsuit. It keeps me from tucking my shirt in and it looks neater." She unbuttoned her jeans, revealing how the black stretchy cotton ran all the way down.

With a swift jerk, he got her jeans down her hips, and she stepped out of them, wearing the sexiest garment he'd ever seen, though she remained mostly covered.

He slid an arm behind her, drawing her to his chest again. Their mouths hovered a fraction apart. When he dipped his hand to her ass, he didn't feel any panty-lines.

"You're not wearing panties." His cock throbbed.

Her breath washed over his lips. "Another benefit of the bodysuit."

Holding her stare, he tugged on the cloth and when she moaned, he realized why. The fabric between her legs applied pressure to her pussy.

Yanking it harder, he watched her eyelids droop over her smoldering gaze as pleasure gripped her. Somehow, teasing her this way had him aching more than if she were nude.

Each slight tug had her rising on her tiptoes and rocking. The sight of the black cloth working between her pussy lips made him burn.

He picked her up and tossed her on the bed. She released a startled gasp that became a cry as he thumbed aside the fabric and found her soaked folds. When he dipped the point of his tongue to her slick heat, she bucked upward. The need to hear her scream his name drove every flick of his tongue.

As he yanked the cloth upward again, it gave way in the crotch. Esme giggled. "It has snaps."

"Easy access." He painted her juices over her seam, up to her clit before enveloping the hard nubbin with his mouth.

She was still coming when he flipped her over, yanked her ass up with an arm under her middle, and drove into her.

Sinking deep, he fell still. She squeezed her eyes shut on the blissful sensation of his hard length stretching her. She hung over his arm, breathing hard.

"Zayden?"

He twitched his hips, raising another moan from her as the head of his cock struck her deeper.

"Hold still. I need a minute." His gruff tone reflected the fact that he struggled not to blow. In response, her pussy squeezed around him.

"Hell." He latched onto her neck and sucked a moment as he churned his hips. She pushed backward. The dam broke loose.

He withdrew slowly, and she cried out. He slammed in again, and she gulped on a moan. Each blinding thrust stole his mind, and he rode the ledge of a cliff so deep, he didn't know if he'd ever find the bottom.

She wrapped her arm across his that banded her middle and linked their fingers. He placed his lips to her ear.

"You're so tight, sweetheart. I can't stop fucking you."

"Don't!"

"Feel my cock stretching your walls? You're getting so slippery for me. God, you're soaked, aren't you?"

The dirty talk made her cry out louder.

"Tell me how good it feels. God…" He growled against her ear.

A ripple of excitement claimed him, and then she clamped down on his thick cock, unearthly noises of ecstasy escaping them both.

Chapter Eleven

Zayden pulled out abruptly, turned her onto her back and kissed her as he drove into her again. The clench and release of her inner walls sucked at him. She was a wild woman in his arms, kissing and rocking with each thrust.

He hooked her ankle over his shoulder, getting a deeper angle, and then it was all over. His roar shook him, and he was helpless against the tumble of feelings accompanying the massive release.

She didn't care that he was a no-good Moon—she gave herself up to him unconditionally. And damn if he hadn't just let the last thread of his heart go from his clutches. It fluttered away, out of grasp, and he looked down into Esme's eyes. What he felt was reflected there.

This wasn't only hot sex with a beautiful woman. She'd captured his heart.

He had no idea how to move forward, though. He didn't do relationships.

Her light touch on his jaw drew a final shudder from him, and he collapsed. They rolled so she was pressed to his side, and he tucked her head under his chin, pinning down her wild curls.

For a moment, he couldn't recall if he'd worn a condom. In the heat of passion, he might have forgotten. But a quick glance down told him he hadn't totally lost his head, and there wouldn't be any little baby Moons being born anytime soon.

She turned her lips into his chest. The caress did more to unseat him from the foundation of everything he knew about the world and himself.

Could he love her right? The way she deserved to be loved? Or was he only setting her up for another failed relationship and broken heart?

He kissed the top of her head. Things had to change in his life if he wanted to keep Esme. Gliding by with odd jobs and putting out the forest fires his father had left behind wouldn't cut it. If he was keeping the ranch, he had to get serious and fast.

Before he knew what he was about to do, he spoke. "My father stole some horses. The sheriff just tracked them to the Moon Ranch."

She stopped drawing a pattern on his chest with her fingertip. "Did you know about the horses?"

"Not 'til today, when I talked to Mimi's great-nephew, who knew about the sale."

"What will you do?"

He sighed. "Try to make it right."

"How do you do that?" She tilted her head to meet his gaze.

"I need to find the money to buy back the horses, then return them to the rancher my father stole them from."

"Can I ask how much?"

He found it didn't bother him as much as he thought it would to confide in her. "Fifteen grand."

She sucked in sharply. "That's a lot."

"It's the only way, though."

"It's honorable."

At that, he barked a laugh. "Nobody's ever called me or any other Moon honorable."

"Then they don't know you."

He hesitated. Should he tell her the rest? "I've had some prior arrests. I've gotten into some fights and —
"

She pressed a fingertip to his lips, halting his words. "I know. You've given the world the middle finger."

He nodded. "You knew about the arrests."

"I've heard rumors but I dismissed them. And the man who's lying here with me right now is telling me that he's screwed up in his past, but I only hear that you're going to spend fifteen thousand dollars to right your father's crime. To me, that says far more than anything you did in your past."

His throat closed off. How could she see any good in him, when he'd struggled all his life to see it in himself?

Maybe it's time I drop the Moon curse and move past it. I'm not my father, and I won't make the same mistakes.

The realization brought the lump higher in his throat, and he swallowed hard.

"Where will you get the money?" she asked.

He sighed. "Dunno. That manager of yours hasn't answered any of my calls. I'm pretty sure he's dismissed me altogether, based on my reputation."

She shook her head, curls tickling across his chest. "That's not right."

"Prejudices in this town run deep against us. Sure, my brothers and I raised hell, but we didn't hurt anyone. I'll have to go to another bank and see what can be done."

Esme pushed onto her elbow to stare down at him. "I think I know a way to get Jason to look again at your application."

He cocked a brow at the devilish gleam that came into her eyes. He'd seen it one other time when she'd negotiated with the homeowner to pay him more.

"Oh hell, I don't like that expression one bit."

She grinned.

"Are you considering blackmail?" he asked. "The manager propositioned you and now you're going to use that leverage to get me a loan?"

"I can't do that. But I can persuade him to take another look at your case."

Thinking about the slimy idiot propositioning her was enough to make his fists clench. "You didn't tell me everything about it, but I'm going to knock his teeth down his throat."

"I won't say he doesn't deserve it."

"What did he do?" He brushed her hair off her cheek.

She chewed her lower lip, still plump from his kisses. "There's a position coming open, and I don't exactly qualify for it, because I didn't finish my degree and they want a college education."

"What did he offer you?" He already fucking knew.

"He said he would tutor me."

"Tutor as in…"

"Yeah. He started out with just telling me it would be some hours each afternoon. But today he told me it would be evenings and weekends too. He is careful not to say he wants to sleep with me, but he doesn't stop staring at my breasts."

Zayden growled.

Esme ran a hand over his chest as if soothing a beast. "What he wants is implied, and I get a bad feeling from the conversations."

"What did you tell him?"

"I told him I was going to think on things, but I never once considered taking him up on his offer."

He issued another low growl. "I'd like to twist off his b—"

"No, you won't. I'll handle this, because it's my problem. Besides, what I'm thinking could benefit me even more in the long run."

He bit back the threat he was about to make and looked down at her. "What are you thinking?"

"That I go back to school. Not an actual college campus, but some online courses to finish my degree. It means passing up this opportunity, but I could find something better in another bank or office somewhere."

"That asshole manager doesn't sound like the best boss to work with anyway."

"He's not. What do you think of my idea?"

Her question was coupled with a crease of worry between her brows. He smoothed his thumb over the wrinkle, heart overflowing with too much emotion to store in his body.

"I think you're brave to change the course of your life."

"I'm not being stupid?"

"Not at all, sweetheart. Daring to dream about having a better life is never stupid."

She eyed him. "You can take your own advice, Zayden."

He chuckled and then slapped her ass lightly. She squealed, and he captured her parted lips with his own.

"Zayden—"

He kissed her again, long and deep, rolling her underneath him to look into her eyes. "I'm not ready to talk about myself in that way. But..."

"But?"

"I'm ready to make you scream my name. And..." he lowered his lips to her ear, "I'm going to suck your wet pussy till you can't think of anything but me. When you come, I'll drive my cock into you and I won't stop until you've given me at least two more orgasms."

"Get another condom," she said breathlessly.

* * * * *

As Mimi took out a spatula to flip the pancakes on the griddle, she sent Zayden a sideways glance. He'd been in her bad graces plenty of times, but the chill coming off the older woman was icier than usual.

He poured himself a mug of coffee and leaned against the counter, watching her. She flipped three pancakes, showing off a perfect light brown on the tops. He sipped. She twisted her mouth in disapproval.

"Spit it out, Mimi. I can see you're dying to tell me off for some thing or other."

She shook her head. "You didn't come home last night."

Zayden's chest swelled with emotion. For the second time in his whole life, he'd spent the entire

212

night holding a woman in his arms — last night and before that, on the mountain.

He'd made love to Esme multiple times too. When he'd woken to find her plastered up against him, her thigh thrown across his hips, he hadn't felt the urge to run out the door. Actually, he'd drawn her closer and kissed her awake, which ended in more mind-blowing sex.

"I was with someone," he said quietly.

Mimi's glance fell on him. "A woman?"

He nodded.

"Well... That's new." Her gaze became more direct.

"It is."

"Do I know her?"

"I'm not sure. Her name's Esme."

"A pretty name."

"Yeah, it is. Mimi, I spoke with Ouray about the horses my father stole. They were sold to a ranch up on the rez. I need fifteen grand to buy them back from him and turn them over to the sheriff."

She switched off the burner under the pancakes and flipped them onto the plate in a short stack. She handed him the plate, and he took it from her, moving to sit at the table while she poured herself coffee and came to sit next to him.

"How will you come up with that sort of money?" she asked.

213

"Dunno. But I can't drag my feet another day. I need to figure out how to raise money and turn a profit on this ranch. You sure my dad didn't have a stash of gold somewhere?"

She gave a rueful chuckle and brought the mug to her lips. "Wish he did. It would make things easier on you."

"On us," he said at once. "You're my family, Mimi, and I'm going to provide a solid home for you for as long as you want to stay."

Tears flooded her eyes, and she reached out to rub his shoulder. "You're a good boy, Zayden. Always have been."

"I'm trying to be a better man."

She nodded. "You've been a ghost of the man you're meant to be for a long time now. I'm glad to hear you're casting off the shadow your father threw on you."

It was his turn to get choked up, but he battled back the emotion and poured maple syrup on his pancakes. After several bites, he turned his head to the window.

"Do you hear an engine in the driveway?"

She nodded and bustled over to look out. For a moment, she was silent, then a shocked gasp escaped her.

He jumped up and joined her at the window. As soon as he spotted the man climbing out of the unfamiliar truck, Zayden strode to the front door. His boots hit the porch, and in the yard, his brother Dane shot him a grin as he slung a duffel over his shoulder.

"Look who turned up, finally. Missed the funeral by about six weeks," he drawled out.

Dane shrugged and mounted the porch steps. They stared each other down. His brother matched him in height and the width of their shoulders was even too. But Zayden felt a lot happier than Dane looked, and that was sayin' a lot.

"Where the hell were ya?" Zayden folded his arms over his chest.

Dane scuffed a boot heel on the worn floorboards. "You won't buy any story I tell ya, so why don't we just say hello and hug like brothers who haven't seen each other in years?"

"Fair 'nough." Zayden stepped forward, arms out. His brother clapped him on the back, and then they drew apart, fists extended. Dane's knuckles grazed his own in their old childish handshake.

"Remember when we thought that was so cool?" Dane asked.

Zayden chuckled. "We were cool."

"Won't argue that." Dane tried for a grin, but the way it faltered made it apparent he didn't feel it deep down.

"Come in. My pancakes are gettin' cold." Zayden turned to the door to find Mimi just beyond the screen, tears running down her face.

Dane saw her and released a whoop of delight. He dropped his duffel and rushed forward. After whipping the screen open, he yanked Mimi into his embrace. She clung to him with a strong grip for a woman of her years.

Zayden watched the welcome and couldn't help but feel warmed by it. They all went inside, and Zayden took up his fork again while Mimi cooked a fresh batch of pancakes for Dane.

"Where's Asher?" he asked.

"Took off again after the funeral."

"He say where?" Dane tucked into his stack with a ton of butter and maple syrup swimming pool at the base of the stack, just like when he was as kid.

"He didn't say." Zayden looked him over. Life in Vegas was right up Dane's alley—the drinking, the night life. But he appeared to be clean and sober right now. Hollows stood under his eyes as if he hadn't been sleeping much, though.

"What happened to you?" he asked his brother.

Dane pressed his lips into a sharp line. "I've been better."

"Where's your wife?" Mimi asked.

His head dropped lower. "Been fightin'. She's staying with a friend, and I figured now was as good a time as any to take a short break and come home."

"A short break," Zayden repeated. "How long you stayin'?"

"I only got a week off work at the club."

Mimi screwed up her face. "You're still working at that club as a dancer?"

He shot her a crooked grin. "You always said I was a dancin' fool, Mimi. Turns out I'm pretty good and women pay me a lot to show them my moves." He writhed a little in his seat, hand on the back of his head.

"Oh you, stop it now." Mimi smacked at him, and he lifted his fork once more.

"So the old man... What happened to him?" Dane looked between them.

"Liver finally gave out. They found him, we buried him. You couldn't get here any sooner?" Zayden arched a brow at Dane.

"I'll be honest—I wasn't in much of a rush to get back. I could do without the lecture now too."

Zayden scanned his brother. "How much money you got on ya?"

Dane drew up straight. "Money?"

"Yeah, how much?"

"What do ya need it for?"

"Look around. This place is crying out for money. Plus, I need to pay off a rancher that Dad screwed over."

Dane blew out a whistle. "Things never change."

"No. But they will now."

"I got a little money, but I don't travel with much. How much are we talkin'?"

"Fifteen grand."

Dane and Mimi recoiled at the figure. "If you got it, I'd appreciate you putting it into the ranch. There's a lot of wrongs to right before I can get started."

"Why don't ya go to a bank?" Dane asked.

"Because I'm askin' you. If you can loan me that amount, then we'll call it your share of the ranch and once I turn a profit, I'll pay you back with a cut of the profits."

Dane stuffed a bite of pancake in his mouth and chewed. "Never figured you for a businessman, Z. Then again, I guess you always had it in ya. You ran this place all those years. Let me see what I can do, okay?"

Zayden nodded. Part of him felt like a shit for asking his brother for money, when they should be sharing happy moments after being apart for years. But fact was, Dane should help the ranch, same as him and even Asher. Next time he talked to his other brother, Zayden planned to ask him for a cut as well. Maybe between the three of them, they could start off with a clean slate and no debt.

Of course, more problems were sure to crop up around here. Things they didn't yet know their father had done.

Later, in the barn, Dane followed him out and leaned against the open door watching Zayden clean stalls.

218

"Make yourself useful," he said to his brother, nodding toward the pitchforks.

He did, working in silence. There was definitely something weighing on him — was it the problem with his marriage? Zayden didn't feel it was his place to pry. He didn't want Dane in his affairs either.

So they worked in silence until the job was done. Then they saddled up and did what they loved to do together — they took to the fields.

* * * * *

"He's in a bad mood today." Natalie's whispered statement sent a bolt of dread through Esme as she stared at Jason's closed office door. He had rushed straight to his office and slammed the door, and nobody had seen him even peep his head out in hours. Usually, during the slower times he would wander out and chat with the tellers, but not today.

She couldn't help but fear she had something to do with his bad mood. Putting him off without an answer was taking a toll on her too, and for totally different reasons. She had no idea if she'd have a job by the end of the day.

He can't fire me for saying no to something unethical in the workplace.

But he could find some silly problem with her performance and write her up for it.

She pressed her lips together and stared at the closed door for a long minute. Then she checked that they didn't have customers before leaving her position and crossing the lobby to his door.

"Esme!" Natalie called from behind her, but she kept walking.

It was best to get this over with.

Drawing herself to her full height, she raised a fist and rapped on the door. He looked up and called, "Come in."

She was holding her breath, so she had to force herself to let it out before entering the office.

Jason sat behind his desk, gaze fixed on her and a wary smile on his face. Before things were said and done, he would get a lot warier...

"Take a seat," he said smoothly.

She perched on the edge of the chair and crossed her legs. He watched her every move. She definitely wasn't reading more into his proposition—the man's tongue was practically hanging out and slobber running down his chin.

He sat back and studied her. "Have you made a decision about the job opening?"

With a little nod, she gathered breath into her lungs—and courage. "I have."

"You're a bright woman. You aren't going to let this chance at a promotion pass. So, when are we going to get started?" He checked his wristwatch. "I should finish up this paperwork in another hour. After that, we should have plenty of time."

Time for him to stare at her breasts and legs. She'd even caught him gawking at her high heels on several occasions, and it made her want to take them off and run out the door.

"Jason, I've decided to pass on your offer."

His face blanked. "You what?"

"I'm passing on the position at this time. The thing is, I'm going back to school, some online night courses so I can get my degree and earn the position myself." She met his eyes with difficulty.

The moment felt like a triumph—not only over men who thought they were owed something in the world, but for herself and how far she'd come in the past few weeks. Being abandoned on that mountain gave her a new look at life and her own role in it. She was no longer a victim of the men around her—she was strong and evicted them from her life because they weren't good for her, no matter their attempts to put pretty icing on the dog turds that they were.

She squared her shoulders and met his gaze head-on. "Give the job to someone more qualified at this time, but I won't be sitting in here with you in the afternoons behind a closed door, Jason."

His face mottled red. "Just what do you think I was offering you?"

She leaned across the desk. "I know what the offer was. You were quite plain. But I won't be falling into that trap. I'm better than that, and I won't compromise myself to get a leg up."

He started shifting files on his desk, but not really doing anything with them. "You've made your choice. I thought you were smarter than that, but—"

She settled back in her seat. "I am smarter. Smart enough to know when my boss is doing something that the HR department of the People's Credit Union would find violates some rules."

Gaze shooting up to hers, his expression hardened. "You misstep and you have no proof."

"You're right—the cameras don't pick up what happens in your office. But the truth has a way of coming out, and you don't really want that."

He narrowed his eyes. "What are you getting at? Are you trying to blackmail me?"

"Not at all. But I would ask a favor of you in exchange for keeping this little... matter... between us."

His chest expanded as he took a deep breath. "What is the favor?"

She smiled, and he winced. It felt good having the upper hand in this case. No wonder women went on full-blown power trips in the workplace. Getting ahead of an asshole boss was equal to sprouting wings and soaring through the sky.

"A man came in about a month ago looking to get a loan against his ranch. You haven't answered him, even though he's submitted all the right paperwork. I'd like for you to give him the attention he deserves and see if he's qualified for the loan."

He eyed her. "You know I can't grant credit to those who don't qualify."

"Of course. I'm not asking you to push him through. I'm asking you to look at his case and give him an answer."

He shifted more files. "Who is he?"

"Zayden Moon."

His head jerked up, and maybe she had some look on her face that shouted to the world that she had feelings for the cowboy, or maybe Jason was just astute enough to read between the lines.

"Fine. I'll have another look at his case."

She nodded. "You'd better have a look at it today, because soon you won't have time with all the interviewing you'll be doing for Roberta's position." She offered him a smile, and he averted his gaze.

Then she stood and walked out of his office, quietly shutting the door behind her.

There—she'd done it. To some, it might not seem monumental to stand up to a boss, but for a woman who'd always deferred to men in her life, it was a bold move. She felt like victory-punching the air.

Natalie and Allison stared at her.

She threw them both a grin and walked back over and unlocked the door with a punch code to get behind the counter again. She smiled to herself. When she'd turned down Jason, his expression had been one of complete shock. The man really was full of himself, wasn't he?

"What was that about?" Natalie asked.

"A work matter. Do you want to take your break first today?" she asked Natalie.

She nodded, still looking at her like she'd grown a second head.

After that, Esme waited on a few customers, and she was still beaming on the inside. She'd taken control not only of her own future but with any luck, her talk with Jason would help Zayden.

She owed him, and for more than saving her from freezing to death on the mountain. He had given her confidence and conviction in herself. Because of Zayden, she saw her own worth now.

First and foremost, she was investing in herself by finishing her schooling. She could do anything she wanted.

All afternoon, she wanted to call Zayden and tell him what had taken place, but she held back. After getting in her car for the ride home, she stared toward the road. She'd never been to the Moon Ranch, but it couldn't be difficult to find. Would Zayden be upset if she just showed up?

The old Esme would call him and ask first. But the new Esme took charge, put the car into gear and headed toward the Moon Ranch.

Stokes, Colorado was a beautiful little town and a tourist trap. But the real draw was the mountains. She hadn't done any winter activities since being stuck on the mountain, but she felt the pull of the rugged world on her senses. The fields and pastures, the jagged peaks of the mountains in the background and the gray winter sky all gave her a feeling of belonging in a way the town never could.

She wished she wasn't wearing a skirt right now, because she'd like nothing more than to slip on an old pair of jeans and boots and take a walk in the open air.

When she reached the road leading to the ranch, she applied the brakes and just sat a moment staring at the sign. Over a rustic arch of wood, it said *MOON RANCH*. Her heart gave a small thump as she realized Zayden was a short distance from her, and this all belonged to him.

She needed to enter his world, to see the problems he was dealing with up close. If they entered a relationship, she had to see the way he lived too. He kept himself closed up — he held back everything. Well, she planned to crack him open, even just a little bit, and then just maybe he'd let her in.

Hopefully coming here this evening showed him how serious she was about him.

The drive curved around the land and ended before a ranch house. The porch needed work and the outbuildings too. The house itself could use a fresh coat of paint and in time a new roof...

No wonder Zayden appeared so overwhelmed. If he didn't have money for the ranch, he had to be stressed.

When she got out and walked up to the house, nobody seemed to be around. She thought of his mother figure, Mimi. Was she inside?

She knocked on the door and waited. A second later, an older woman with stark white hair opened the door.

She looked Esme over, taking in the red coat she wore over her business attire and down to her sensible boots she changed into after work.

"Can I help you?" she asked.

"Um..." She wrapped the coat more tightly around herself as a gust of wind struck her. "I'm a friend of Zayden's."

Her eyes zeroed in on her. She was being sized up. Esme waited for the assessment to pass and smiled at Mimi.

She cocked her head like a little bird. "You're the woman he's been seeing and spent the night with."

A flush hit her cheeks. "Yes."

"Come inside out of the wind. He's out on the ranch somewhere with his brother."

Esme blinked. She knew Zayden had brothers, but none that were around right now. It shouldn't bother her that she didn't know very much about him, but it did, and that was because she wanted more with Zayden. She wanted him to let her into his life.

Mimi offered to take her coat, and she slipped off her snow-covered boots out of respect for the clean but worn floors.

"Come into the kitchen. Do you drink tea or coffee?"

"Either is fine, thank you." She followed the woman through the house. There weren't photos like in other homes. No family history, no reminder of a love shared here. It gave her a sad pang.

The kitchen was much homier, with a pot of soup simmering on the stove and a crisp stack of white dishtowels on the counter. Mimi offered her a smile. "Have a seat while I get the kettle on. What did you say your name is?"

"Esme."

"Pretty name." The woman turned into profile, and right away Esme picked up the woman had some Native American blood coursing through her veins. That proud, strong profile and the white hair harkened to some other world, and Esme felt herself sinking under the spell of being in this woman's presence.

As she looked around, the ranch grew more charming. Though Zayden and his brothers had lived a hard life here and would probably beg to differ, Esme saw nothing but potential.

The woman smiled at Esme for the first time. "My boys call me Mimi."

She nodded. "I heard."

Her brows shot up. "Zayden spoke of me?"

"A little, yes. But Zayden doesn't say much at all, does he?"

"You do know my Zayden then." She chuckled and put away the stack of towels. Then she pulled down two blue pottery mugs from a shelf and dropped teabags into each.

Esme's heart warmed a bit. Did she know Zayden? In some regards, yes. She knew he was strong and determined. He didn't have a problem with telling people like it was. But when in bed with the cowboy, she sensed a tenderness that she hadn't known with other men, men who professed to love her.

"Tell me about yourself. What do you do? Do you live in town?" Mimi got out a plastic box and pulled a couple muffins from the depths. She set these on a plate and then placed them on the table in front of Esme.

"These look delicious. You made them?" The crumb topping and fat blueberries enticed her more than any bakery muffin from town that tourists spent too much for.

"Of course I did. Picked those blueberries myself back in the summer. I freeze them for the winter months. The picking was hard this year. Lots of bears wanted my berries, but I won some in the end." She smiled, and Esme couldn't help but return it.

"I do live in town. I work at the credit union."

"But you aren't originally from Stokes."

"No." She shook her head, thinking of the silly tale of following her ex there and getting dumped. Her past seemed like a trail of decisions made by a young and inexperienced girl, including her time with Owen. But she felt different now.

"How did you meet Zayden?"

She met the woman's eyes. "He rescued me off the mountain about six weeks back."

"That was you! How horrible for you. What an ordeal. These storms are nothing to play with."

"I found that out myself. Thank goodness Zayden was there."

"Ask Zayden and he'll tell you he's purely selfish, but that man will stand up to a grizzly for someone. He's scrappy and smart, even though he never finished high school."

A pang of sadness hit Esme. The man had missed out on untold possibilities, hadn't he? And he never said a word about his plight, just kept fighting for what he wanted, which right now was the ranch.

"Nobody knows that mountain like Zayden, so luck was on your side that day, Esme." Mimi smiled. Just then the kettle whistled, and she got up to fetch it off the burner. After she poured both mugs, she returned with them to the table and went after sugar and milk.

When they settled with their hot drinks, they looked to each other.

"I hope Zayden isn't upset with me for coming here uninvited."

Mimi waved a hand in dismissal. "He's more bark than bite."

A smile spread over her face at the woman's opinion of the man she knew far better than Esme did. How much would she learn by sitting here over tea with this sweet woman?

"Help yourself to a muffin. You just got off work and must be hungry."

After plucking one from the plate, she peeled back the paper wrapper and took a bite. The sweet and buttery flavors melded on her tongue. After swallowing, she said, "It's even more delicious than it looks!"

Mimi beamed. "More where those came from. Better eat them before Z comes in and devours the whole container." She chuckled.

"Z?" Delight hit her at the nickname.

"His brothers Dane and Asher called Zayden that from a young age."

She considered the nickname and found it suited the rough cowboy.

Mimi nibbled on a muffin too, but Esme noted she kept glancing toward the window.

"I'm interrupting your day," she said.

Mimi shook her head. "Not at all. You've given me a small break, and I thank you for it. I was just wondering when those two Moons would turn up. They rode out hours ago, and it's pretty dark now."

Esme's stomach hollowed at the thought of Zayden getting into some trouble in this weather and at night too. It must have shown on her face, because the older woman reached over and touched the back of her hand.

"They'll be fine now — don't you worry. One time Zayden heard tell of a steer that got separated from the herd. The cowpokes who worked here on the ranch weren't having any luck and next thing I knew, Zayden was missing."

"How old was he?" She cradled her mug to get some warmth back into her fingers after the shock of worry. Too well she knew how easy it was to get into a bad situation and have no way out. She'd learned that the hard way after leaving that cabin. But Zayden had shared the story of running away to the mountain at age eleven. He was resourceful, like Mimi said.

"At only fourteen, he rode out without any of us knowing. Nobody knew where he'd gone but his brother Dane, and he confided after I gave him a stern talkin' to. See, a bad storm loomed over us and none of them should have been out in it, but a steer means a lot of money to a rancher, and well... Zayden acted as the rancher from a very young age. He was in charge, you see."

She was getting a clear picture in her mind, of a young boy who'd shouldered so much responsibility, who hadn't been able to finish school because of it perhaps. And who'd grown hardened to life because of it.

She nodded so Mimi would continue.

"He was out for hours, and the cowpokes went after him, of course. But the thing about Zayden is he's a risk-taker. He doesn't think about himself either. He just barrels in with guns blazing, and to hell with the consequences."

"Like he found me. He looked on the other side of the mountain."

She nodded. "He knows more about the outdoors than most, and he deserves to be the true owner of this ranch now. Though his brothers will always share a part in it, he's the one who will take charge."

"Did he find the steer?"

"Yep, and he led it all the way home through the snow. He was exhausted and half-frozen, but he did the job he'd set out to do, and I was mighty proud of him."

Esme warmed from the tale. And it made her feel closer to the man who'd jumped into her life and changed her thinking about how she should be treated by men.

"He's a good man," she said quietly.

"Few better." Mimi eyed her. "Don't let his gruff exterior put you off. Inside, he's a softy. But he won't show it to you easy. In fact, he'll probably fight you tooth and nail to avoid it."

That brought a smile to her lips. "I know..."

Memories of their argument outside the pizza joint solidified what Mimi was telling her. He cared for her but wouldn't let her know. He held everything inside.

"It's the way he was raised," Mimi added as if knowing her train of thought. "There wasn't much love for those boys, and that's a damn shame. I did my best with them, but Zayden was thirteen before he hired me—"

"Wait—hired you?"

Mimi gave her a rueful smile. "Yes, that boy took charge of the ranch and his brothers. Knew he was over his head and went out and hired two ranch hands and came up to the rez asking for help. I came down the mountain and never looked back."

Heart sore at what Zayden and his brothers had faced, she could look at Mimi and see what a good woman she was. Inside and out.

"They're like my own," Mimi said softly.

"I can see that." She reached across the table and squeezed the woman's hand, small and hard with work. "Thank you for telling me about this." She opened her mouth to say more, but at that moment, a thump sounded, and both of them looked up to see the door filled with a muscled cowboy.

Hat dipped low, his gaze was barely visible as it swayed from Mimi to Esme. She squeezed her thighs together as a jolt of wanting hit at the mere sight of Zayden.

"You all right?" he grated out.

"Of course." She got to her feet and circled the table to approach him. He carried with him the cold wind lingering on his heavy coat, and snow dusted the tops of his boots, though it looked as if he'd stomped them off before entering the house.

"I hope you don't mind that I came here without talking to you first," she said.

"No." His gaze fell on her, infusing her with warmth, but he didn't smile. The man's smiles were so rare, and all she wanted in life was to put more of them on his handsome face.

He looked past her to Mimi, who still sat cradling her tea. "You seen Dane?"

She blinked and then went pale. "Isn't he out with you?"

"He came back over an hour ago. I got some trouble—a winter calf. The cows weren't separated when they shoulda been, and now we'll have a little one on the ground in the dead of winter."

Mimi stood. "I didn't hear Dane come inside, but maybe he did."

"His truck's gone. Mimi, will you check if his clothes are too?"

She nodded and quickly moved out of the kitchen, squeezing past Zayden and touching his arm as she went.

"Your brother?" Esme asked.

He gave a nod. "I got more to worry about right now than that dumb ass." He looked her over, taking in her work attire, and his eyes narrowed. "How strong are you?"

Chapter Twelve

"He's gone." Mimi returned with tears in her eyes.

"Goddamn him." Since he couldn't smash his brother's nose with his fist, Zayden clenched his jaw. "He must have come back to the house, got his things while you didn't notice and drove out."

Mimi nodded, and Esme moved to the woman and slipped an arm around her. Zayden watched the exchange with shock and a thumping heart. Whatever had taken place in this kitchen over cups of tea had bonded the women — and he couldn't help but feel a flood of warmth at the knowledge.

He eyed Esme again. "I could use your help, if you're willin'."

She looked up into his eyes. "Anything."

"Mimi, do you got some of those coveralls you wear in the barn for her to put on? She doesn't want to ruin her pretty outfit helpin' me pull a calf."

She blinked. "Pull..." Her lips parted on an O of surprise, and then her shoulders drew back and she nodded. "I'll do what I can to help."

God, she was prettier than ever and standing in his kitchen. The fact that she'd come all the way up here just to see him made him wonder if she really had trouble with that dickhead boss of hers, but there'd be plenty of time for conversation during the birthing.

Mimi took her away to get changed, and he watched them go. He wandered to the window to look out into the night. He couldn't see any vehicles parked out front, but he'd already searched for Dane's and knew he was gone. Damn him. He'd breezed in and out so fast, and Zayden was mad at himself for believing he might stay on for good and shoulder the burden of the Moon Ranch alongside him.

Guess he was wrong.

No time for dwelling on things he had no control over. If he'd learned anything growing up, it was that. He couldn't stop Dane from leaving any more than he could make his dad quit the whiskey.

"She's a bit taller than I am, but the coverall still fits her." Mimi's announcement made him turn to see them entering the room. Esme's curves were concealed by the long-sleeved one-piece garment, and he was quickly learning what a turn-on it was when he couldn't see all of her, but knew what would be waiting for him later.

His cock twitched behind his fly. He would be hard-pressed to keep his hands off her, but they had work to do.

"Here, you'll need this." Mimi handed her a knit hat and gloves. Esme pulled the hat down over her curls and looked up at him.

Beautiful.

He drew a deep breath and nodded to her to take the leather work gloves Mimi offered. "Come on."

"Take my coat. Don't get your beautiful red one covered in muck," Mimi called after them. In the mudroom, he paused while she put her own snow boots back on and then gave her Mimi's coat.

"You gonna be okay with this?" He wanted nothing more than to cup her delicate jaw, lean in and kiss her.

"Yes. I'm ready."

He led the way to the barn. The cow stood in the center of the space, tail straight out as she bore down on the calf that refused to come.

"Found her separated from the herd. They'd moved on to graze a ways, and I knew by the way she was actin' that a calf was comin'. Damn my father for not separatin' them."

The oath was lost in the sound of the animal mooing loudly.

He walked up to her and patted her side. "We're here to help. Hold on and we'll get it out."

Esme stood nearby, looking uncertain. "I've never been around such a large animal before. Horses seem different somehow."

He nodded. "I'll get the calf puller ready, but I'm hopin' a rope works. And I can't get the vet up here, when I still owe her money."

He worked quickly, giving Esme directions to grab some extra hay and spread it in one of the center stalls, nice and thick to counteract the drafts.

"It's March—isn't it close enough to spring for the baby to survive?" she asked as she scattered the hay.

"If we keep it warm 'til the weather breaks." He shed his coat and rolled his shirt sleeve up as far as he could to his shoulder. Then he positioned himself behind the cow and slowly reached inside the birth canal.

A loud moaning moo sounded at the invasion, and he soothed the animal with quiet words as he explored the inside.

The baby moved against his hand, and a pang of excitement hit him. At least it wasn't dead. Yet.

Esme returned to his side. "What can I do to help?"

"Keep her still. Just kind of lean into her flank there, but if she starts to go over, you jump out of the way fast. Can't have you getting crushed. And grab that rope I put around her. I'm going to try to find the calf's forelegs and straighten them out so the baby can slip free. I think it's legs are tucked under." His voice came in bursts as he explored using only his sense of touch.

It was hard to tell what body part was what, but when he ran his fingers over what he thought was the calf's shoulder, it sucked his finger.

He gave a sharp laugh.

"What is it?" Esme leaned away from the cow's head to look at him.

"It sucked my finger."

"It's alive!"

"Very much. Let's see if we can move these legs around now." A contraction had the cow's body clamping down around his arm, and he quickly pulled it free to keep from being bruised. When it was over, he reached in again. This time he found one of the front legs tucked underneath the body of the calf.

With gentle force, he tugged it outward. Finding the other leg was trickier, and he feared the calf would expire before he located it.

The cow wobbled on its feet, and he jerked his head up to look at Esme. "Get outta the way!"

She quickly leaped back just as the cow toppled over, too tired to continue.

"Dammit." He stood back, panting, staring at the huge animal lying on its side.

Esme dropped to her knees. "Is it trapped now? Impossible?"

"No, this is better. Now we got leverage against her body. I have to find that other leg." He dove back in, feeling with his eyes closed for a long minute. "Ah-ha!"

"You got it?"

"Got it. Get me that rope." He pulled both front hooves out of the momma's body, and Esme squealed.

"It's so tiny!"

"Yeah, hope it ain't early. That reduces its chances of survival. All right, the rope now, sweetheart."

She passed it into his hands and sat back on her haunches to watch him loop it around the small hooves.

He looked at her face, bright with excitement, and felt a stirring of such love that it froze him for a moment. He stared at her. She stared back.

Hell. He'd fallen for her.

Too late—he'd figure it out later. Right now, he had work to do.

* * * * *

The glow in Zayden's eyes had her heart pounding triple time, and she could barely draw breath. All this time she'd known there was more than just lust and attraction between them, but looking at Zayden now and seeing that gleam of love in his eyes... Well, if she could take off soaring into the sky with joy, she would.

As the cow gave a long moan, she became grounded once more, standing on solid earth and watching her man battle to save a calf that shouldn't be born at this time of year.

He scooted back on the floor, rope wrapped around his fists.

"Can I help you pull?"

"Might not need ya to. Let's see." With that, he dug in his boot heels and pushed himself backward. The calf's hooves moved a few inches outward but were sucked back in most of the way when he let up.

Esme watched the progress in awe. If anybody had told her when she'd moved to Stokes that this would be where she ended up — or that she'd stop being able to picture herself anywhere else, with any other man — she would have laughed at them. But watching Zayden's determined pulls and the fierce expressions cross his face, she knew this was it for her.

The calf's forelegs appeared to the joints.

"You've got to be tired. Let me pull with you." She didn't wait for his response, just crouched near him and took hold of the rope above his fists. Soon they got a rhythm going, and all of a sudden, she toppled back into him. Fluids and something solid hit her legs, and she twisted to see the calf was out.

He scrambled forward to get the rope off its legs then he stuck his fingers into its nose to clear away some of the fluids.

"Grab that blanket and rub it hard. We need it to take a breath. God knows how long it was stuck."

She rushed for the blanket. Rubbing down the calf was something she'd never done in her life, and she put all her concentration into getting it dry.

"C'mon! Breathe." He slapped it a couple times.

Esme watched its rib cage for movement but saw nothing. Yet its eyes were open and blinking, the lashes insanely long.

"Come on, baby!" She rubbed it using both hands and the blanket. Zayden added his efforts and when it dragged in a small breath, Esme burst out laughing in relief.

"It's breathing," she cried.

"Lemme have the blanket." He took it from her hands and continued massaging the calf as it took more and more breaths.

The cow shifted, and before Esme knew what was going to happen, the momma was on its feet and leaning over her calf to clean her.

Zayden stepped back to let nature take over. Esme moved to his side. She couldn't stop herself from leaning against him, despite what filth covered them both.

He put an arm around her back and kissed the top of her hat. "You were fantastic."

"You did most of the work," she said.

"You make an excellent rancher." His words trailed off as he stared into her eyes.

She felt like that calf, unable to draw a full breath as she gazed up at him. "Zayden..."

"I want to kiss you, but I don't want to touch you 'til my hands are clean."

"Oh, who cares?" She threw her arms around his neck, and he caught her against him, tight. The moment their lips met, she gave up all ideas of walking away from this man. She loved him, and she was going to fight for them as hard as they'd just fought for that calf to be born.

He brushed his lips over hers with an indescribable tenderness. When he pulled back, he continued to nuzzle her. "You smell bad."

She laughed. "So do you."

"Stay with me tonight." His gruff words were a whisper that sent her heart hammering faster.

"I have work in the morning."

"Wake up early then. But don't go."

A lump of emotion and love filled her throat. She nodded. How could she say no to that?

When he drew away to check the animals, she watched him. Knowing full well what she was feeling in her heart showed plain on her face and not caring one bit. The calf remained lying down with the momma's tongue stroking over its back to stimulate and clean it.

"They'll be all right. I think I'll leave them here for a bit and check on them later to see if they'll move into the stall where it's less drafty."

She slipped her gloved hand around his upper arm. "They'll be all right?"

"Yeah. Let's get inside and clean up." When he turned to her, his eyes glimmered with that lust that had started everything.

"Will Mimi mind if we shower together? Or I spend the night?"

"Even though my dad was alive, she'd been alone a long time. She likes having me here and I can tell she likes your company too."

She smiled. "I'm glad. I like her."

"She's a dear woman."

Esme took in his face as he spoke the words sounding so unusual from his hard lips. Mimi was right—Zayden was tough and kept everything inside, but this glimpse she had right now was enough to make her fall even deeper in love with the man.

They left the barn and he led her in through the back door of the house to a utility room. A washer and dryer stood quiet for the night, but everything smelled of fresh detergent and dryer sheets. She stripped off her gloves and coat, tugging up her sleeves to wash off in the utility sink. Zayden waited his turn, stripping to the waist and shucking his heavy boots.

She shook the water from her fingers and tracked his movements as he scrubbed to the shoulders and rinsed the soap from his skin.

"That's good enough till we get to the shower." There it was—that crooked grin, a direct line straight to her soul.

She slipped her hand into his, and he led her through the dark house.

* * * * *

Each swirl of the washcloth over Esme's spine made her shiver, and he couldn't stop himself from doing it one more time.

Her lush, water-drenched hip brushed against his stiff cock, and he groaned. She twisted her face and smiled as she did it again.

"You're asking for it," he growled.

"You got the hint?"

That was it—he picked her up, legs around his hips, and pressed her against the wall. Her slick heat tormented him, and all he wanted was to sink into her bareback.

Would she let him fill her, claim her in all ways?

His brain misfired—the last thing he needed was someone else to take care of. Yet, the thought of Esme walking out of his life hurt.

Hell, he loved her. He'd known it a while now, and tonight had fused all those moments they'd shared into one big one that had taken over his whole life.

He couldn't be dumb and believe this could go further. But for tonight, he refused to let her go.

When she kissed him, the passion flowed as hot as the water. He ground against her, raising a moan to her lips in answer. The blast of sensation stole his mind a moment, and he almost plunged into her tight heat.

Shaking, he lowered her toes to touch the shower floor and switched off the water. She stepped out and gave him a crook of her finger. He stood motionless as she spread a towel on the countertop and hitched herself onto it.

"I don't have a condom in here," he grated out.

"I'm not asking you to fuck me." She arched a brow. "You know what to do."

She parted her thighs, the wetness coating her folds an invitation to his tongue. With a low growl, he dropped to his knees and sank his tongue into her pussy. She clasped the back of his head and pushed him deeper inside her. God, this woman was killing him. His cock couldn't get harder, bouncing on his abs and dripping pre-cum.

He licked a path up her soaking seam to her clit. The nubbin strained, plump and juicy, and he sucked it between his lips. She squelched a moan and rocked forward to meet his tongue. He flicked her clit with short strokes, and she was already peaking.

Hell, he wasn't going to last. Reaching down, he closed his fist around his cock and squeezed. Need washed up from the base of his spine, sensation doubling when Esme came apart for him.

Her gasps punctuated her pulsations, and he sucked on her clit harder, drawing a quiet groan from her.

When she tugged his hair, he drew back to look into her eyes. "Can I take you to bed?"

She smiled. "You're asking?"

"What I want to do to you there requires some consent."

She shuddered and ran a hand between her breasts. "I can't wait…"

He drew her off the sink and wrapped the towel around her. He didn't bother with one for himself, just opened the door, looked up and down the hall to make sure Mimi wasn't standing there, and crossed the two steps to his bedroom.

As soon as they stepped through the door, he closed it and swept her into his arms. She hooked her legs around his waist and kissed him. The desire rolled off her like heat waves.

When he lay her down on the bed, he reached into his bedside drawer. She watched him with burning eyes, the intensity getting to him more than the sight of her nudity ripe for the taking.

He drew out a condom — and a length of rope.

She sucked in a sharp breath. "What do you plan on doing with that?"

"I'm going to tie you up and have my way with you. Do you trust me?"

248

"Zayden…" Her stomach dipped as he stretched the hemp between his hands.

"You can say no. But I've always wanted to take a woman with her hands bound and make her scream."

Another shiver coursed through her. He settled his steady gaze on her, waiting for her to make a choice. If she said no, he'd still take her — he couldn't deny her or his own need. But adding in the rope… Well, his cock pulsed at the thought of her handing over all trust to him, of putting herself entirely in his hands.

After a moment, she didn't reply, and he tossed down the rope, reaching for the condom instead.

"No," she rasped, leaning upward. Her wrists outstretched. "I want it. I trust you. I-I…love you, Zayden."

Not many people in this world could make his jaw drop, but she did. He gazed down at her beautiful face and wondered how the hell he deserved such a thing as love.

"You don't have to say it back. I just want you. I want this." She thrust her wrists forward more.

His chest exploded with so much emotion that it stole his thought. He had no memory of grabbing the rope or knotting it around her hands so she couldn't move but still had blood flow.

Then he pressed a hand to her stomach, and she laid down for him.

"Spread your legs."

"Oh God." Her soft cry spoke of how turned on she was. As if he couldn't see her soaking wet folds for himself.

He pumped his cock once and then covered it in a condom. He planned to tease and torment her before he took his own pleasure, but he wanted to be ready when he did.

She watched with eyelids drooping over her smoldering green eyes.

"How did we get from the mountain to this?" she whispered.

His heart hurt from so much love leaking from it. "You were sent to me," he said thickly.

The shine of her eyes revealed tears, and he leaned in to brush his lips across hers. The gentle caress tugged at his guts more, and he closed his eyes as he deepened the kiss. It spiraled out of control, their tongues entwined and soft moans filling the room.

When he tore free, he kissed down her throat, nipping at her flesh as he did. Damn if he didn't want to mark the woman — make her his. He was probably a freaking head-case, but right now, he couldn't stop.

She lay there staring up at him, her heart in her eyes, as he kissed down her body, circling each nipple with his tongue before giving each a long, sucking pull into his mouth. She arched upward, writhing, hands bound before her.

Moving downward, he lapped a trail to her pussy once more. This time, she bit back a scream as he thrust his tongue deep.

Chapter Thirteen

Her senses were firing off like cannons on a warship, and she could barely see straight as Zayden licked her pussy till her previous orgasm seemed like a small blip on the radar. She succumbed to his lips and tongue, and each time he tongued her channel, she felt a frenzy rise up in her.

She couldn't even touch him, and somehow that knowledge amped up their lovemaking. The rope came as a shock to her, but she saw the need in the man—he needed her to give herself up to him, to trust unconditionally.

And she did.

She trusted him with her life, with her body and now her soul.

Without warning, he thrust two fingers into her pussy. She bucked, thighs trembling. The first wave of release hit, and she felt helpless now, rolling in a sea of bliss.

She stifled her cries, and Zayden dragged more from her. When the slick sounds of her release on his fingers filled the room, she looked into his eyes.

"Please."

He hovered over her and gave his cock a long stroke from root to tip. The purple head encased in latex swelled even more, and she wet her lips. "If I bind your ankles too?"

A quiver of excitement struck. "Do it," she whispered.

He fished in his drawer again, coming out with more rope. The scratchy fibers against her bare skin only heightened her need, and soon she was writhing, bound hand and foot, at Zayden's total mercy.

She knew he'd die before he let anything happen to her, and that was what this moment came down to. He was showing her he loved her as much as she loved him.

His gaze raked over her, head to foot and slowly back up. When he leaned over her, she bucked upward to capture his lips. The kiss lingered, a light brushing of mouths that said so much more.

"I need you," he grated out.

"I'm yours to take."

He pinned her in his stare. "You have no idea what that does to me."

She wet her lips. "Show me then."

* * * * *

In one hard thrust, he sank balls deep. The exquisite heat encompassed his whole body, and he could only think about getting deeper, closer, into her sweet body.

When he took her bound wrists and wrapped them around the back of his neck, she gave a soft mewl against his throat. He began to move. Churning his hips, he brought another moan from her, and he answered with his own as he withdrew his cock.

Each inch he sank into her, he lost himself more. All because the woman had been lost on the mountain and he'd been playing hero. What was it inside him that urged him to save people? First his family. Then hearing Esme was on the mountain, lost and alone, he hadn't stopped to think of his actions, only gone up after her.

What he'd come down with was a soft woman who had seen her share of heartache. But that was over now. She had him.

Does that mean she won't have more heartache?

Not if you don't break her heart, asshole. So don't.

He caught her lips in a long kiss, and their bodies moved in slow, sexy rhythm. He plunged into her again, feeling her walls tighten around his length. He couldn't hold on much longer. The feel of the rope against his nape made his balls throb. She wasn't the only one tethered — the little woman had his heart in her hands.

She bit at his lower lip, and he growled at the sharp sting. He returned the favor, making her pussy clamp down hard on him.

"More… oh God…" Her sweet cries fell on his ears.

The need drove them on, and the moment she gave herself up to him again, he let go. A searing heat shot through his groin, and he exploded with jets of cum.

She held onto him, riding out the waves as her own orgasm pulsated through her. He stared down at her, raking in the sight of the damp curls on her forehead, her swollen lips. God, she belonged to him, right here and now.

A final shudder ran up his spine, and he collapsed. Breathing hard, he closed his eyes and buried his face against her fragrant neck. Moments passed, and he rolled to the side and began untying her hands. When the rope fell away, he massaged her wrists and looked into her eyes.

"Okay?"

She nodded.

He did the same for her ankles, and then stretched out and pulled her flush against him, stroking her wild curls and thinking of all that had happened today. His brother coming, finding the cow about to birth and getting it home, the fury pounding through him at the sight of Dane's truck being gone and finally, walking into the house to see Esme.

"The best end to a calf birthing I've ever had," he rumbled.

She broke into giggles and slapped at his chest. "I hope so!"

He caught her hand and enfolded it in his. "What made you come to the ranch in the first place?"

She went still, and his stomach knotted.

"Was it that asshole boss of yours?"

She nodded against his chest. "I did what I set out to do."

"What was that?" He waited for her answer, with no idea which way this could go.

"I turned down the job and his offer to 'tutor' me."

He didn't realize he'd been holding his breath 'til he let it out. "Good."

"And I...I might have blackmailed him a little."

He jerked. Catching her chin in his fingers, he drew her face up to meet her gaze. "What did you do? The loan?"

She laughed again. "I only asked for something in return for not turning him into HR."

He groaned.

"I asked him to quit putting off your loan application and look at it again."

God, she was perfect. "You didn't do that for me, did you?"

"Yup."

"You could have been fired on the spot. Esme —"

She put a fingertip over his lips, ending his sentence. "I told you — I love you. And I didn't ask him to approve you on my behalf. It's only right that he looks at the loan application. My guess is he was just being a dick, ignoring you because he was on some power trip. I put a stop to that."

He shook his head. "You have guts, woman. I knew it from the first time I saw you, but you keep surprising me every day."

"Did I surprise you today?"

His brows shot up. "Hell yeah. You stood up to that fuckhead and then came looking for me."

"I hate to break it to you, Z, but looking for you isn't very scary. You don't frighten me, even with all the growls and glares in your arsenal. You—"

"What did you call me?" He stared at her.

A pink glow hit her cheeks. "Uh…Z. Mimi called you that. If you don't want me to, I won't."

His heart flexed. The nickname was one of the fonder memories he had of being on the Moon Ranch. His brothers teasing him, Mimi calling him home for supper and the warmth the four of them created as a makeshift and somewhat wounded family while his father was passed out drunk in parts unknown.

He squeezed her hand. "Z is fine, sweetheart. And maybe it's time I admit something to you, since you've been nothing but open with me."

"And I did let you tie me up," she added with a twinkle in her eyes.

His lips tipped up. "You did. And I hope you'll let me again. But that isn't what I was going to tell you. I wanted to say…" Now that the moment was on

257

him, the admission paused on his lips, and he wasn't able to say the words. Could he?

He sighed. She waited while he struggled.

"Not many are close to me. Almost no one," he said.

She nodded. "I know."

"But you are. I wasn't looking for it, but you curled yourself up in my arms and it didn't take long for me to start lovin' you."

She blinked rapidly as tears hit her eyes. "Zayden..."

"I love you, sweetheart. You deserve better, but... Well, from this day on, I'll try my best to be a better man for you."

"I...I can't believe you're telling me this."

"You deserve to hear it. I love you, Esme." He tipped her face up to his and kissed her. The soft kiss turned to more, and soon she was sliding a condom on his hard length and sinking over him nice and slow.

* * * * *

Come morning, she was gone. He woke to the scents of frying sausage and knew Mimi had breakfast cooking and that Esme had left while it was still dark to head back home and get ready for work.

He sat up, saw the rope laying on the floor and burned for her.

His words to her the previous night hadn't all been true. He did love her—wanted her bad. But having a relationship was out of the question.

He got up and dressed, trying to ignore the scent of her on his skin. Then he slipped out to the barn before Mimi could call him into the kitchen for breakfast. Morning had dawned brighter, with more warmth in the air, and he inhaled deeply as he crossed the yard to the barn.

The calf was on its feet, nursing from its momma, and he issued a sigh of relief at the sight. Neither had died during the night, and things would probably work out—for the animals, at least.

Esme was another story.

What had possessed him to say those things to her? To make promises he couldn't keep? Hell, he couldn't be a better man if he tried. He bore the name of Moon—bad enough—but now he was saddled with a failing ranch and no life to speak of to share with her.

Doing his chores sank him into a deeper rut of a bad mood, and by the time he stomped back to the house, he ground his teeth too.

Mimi poked her head into the living room as he entered. "Where's that woman of yours? Did you lose her already?"

The teasing tone rubbed him totally wrong. "She's not my woman and she went home to change and go to work today."

259

Mimi narrowed her eyes at his snapping tone. "What did you do, Zayden Moon?"

He winced at both the tone and the reminder of who he was. "I didn't do anything. I just realized…"

For the first time in forever, he felt like a child under Mimi's scrutiny. No one dared to question him in so long that he was nudged off balance. But it was still his life, and he was in control, goddammit.

He headed past her into the kitchen, and she stepped aside, but as soon as he poured his coffee, she got in his face again.

"You feel something for her, and you're going to push her away."

"I can't be saddled with more to take care of."

"Seems like she can handle herself, and you're just the frosting on the cake."

He averted his gaze from the woman who felt close enough to him to even bring up the topic and face his wrath if things went south during the discussion. He took a sip of coffee, not tasting it at all.

"I can't be responsible for her too. I've spent my life being there for everyone around me."

Mimi planted a hand on her narrow hip and gave him that straight-shooter glare that not one Moon boy wanted back in the day. "Weren't you off for the past decade satisfying your own whims, Zayden? Or have you got a wife and kids hidden somewhere I don't know about?"

"You know I don't." He set aside his mug a little too hard, and coffee sloshed over the top onto the counter.

Mimi went on. "You picked her. I saw the way you walked across the yard after birthin' that calf too."

He jerked, jarred that she had looked out the window at them and seen something he didn't want to admit to now.

"She's in love with you." Mimi went to the stove and flipped French toast onto a plate for him, and then she held it out like she wanted to do him bodily harm.

He sighed and took the plate. Not remotely hungry, he still made a stab at the fluffy toast and tried to appease Mimi.

She leaned against the counter, staring at him without pause. "You tell her you love her too?"

He almost bit through the tines of his fork. Sending her a glare, he grumbled, "Yeah, I did. But I can still take it back. There's time for her to get away from me."

Mimi barked out a laugh that sounded much larger than her slight frame. "You can take something like that back, can you? You're the last person I'd ever believe could scoff off love, Z. For a boy who had little and a man who's had none, you sure—"

He slammed down his fork and jumped to his feet. "Stop riding me, woman!"

"Woman? That's right, go on with your sassy mouth and tell me how you feel about me while you're at it—or take it all back, why don't you? Tell me that I wasn't really needed here on the ranch all those years. That you never needed a soft word or kindness because you're a no-good, hard-headed, rotten-souled Moon."

"Don't. Mimi—"

"If you won't deny your terrible parentage, then at least don't deny the good that's in you too, boy." She stepped up to him and smacked him square in the chest. He rocked on his boots from shock, not from her strength. The woman barely reached his shoulder, but she was an Ute and had the strength of character of a warrior.

Her blue eyes burned into him. "Tell me that you don't love her and want a life with her. Then I'll hold up a mirror to your face and call you a liar!"

"Fine! I love her. I fucking *want* her—by my side and in my life."

"But you won't fight for her. You want to give her up."

"No, dammit, I don't want to give her up. She's one of two people who loved me despite who I am."

"Who's the other?" she pressed.

"You." He bit off the word and added a glare at her.

"Maybe neither of us love you despite who you are—we love you for *who* you are. Time for that

262

mirror." She grabbed his arm and dragged him across the kitchen to a small mirror on the wall, one of the few things that his old man hadn't smashed over the years in a drunken rage.

She towed him up in front of it. "Look at your reflection."

The command made him sag at the knees to see his whole face. God, he felt stupid right this minute, but he couldn't deny the only person who had been there for him, had picked right up where they left off the moment he set foot on this ranch.

He peered at his own face. Some of his ma, some of his pa. A few lines around his eyes and a scar on his cheekbone from a sucker punch he'd taken in an alley one night. The guy hadn't walked away with only one scar, he was certain of that.

He also saw the beard stubble that Esme loved searing across her inner thighs and the thick hair she tangled her fingers in to bring him down for a kiss. It might not be a face a mother could love, but it was a face that a woman did.

Mimi saw the moment the realization dawned on him, and she released his arm and stepped back with a nod of her head.

"Dammit. Don't look so smug. And I'm sorry for callin' you woman. I know how you hated that disrespect." He turned to her, feeling thirteen again. He hadn't taken to being parented at that time of his life either, but now he was old enough to see she meant the best for him.

"If you love her, don't let her go for all the wrong reasons. You aren't your daddy or even your brothers, and it pains me to say that, but neither of them stuck around for you, did they? Now, what I see before me is a strong and resourceful man who doesn't always go about things the conventional way, but you get things done and if someone's on your good side, well then they get the heart of gold." She punched his chest again.

This time he laughed. "Damn, Mimi, your knuckles have gotten bonier over the years."

"Nah, I'm just stronger now. Either sit and finish your breakfast or take yourself off and see to that woman and this ranch. You hear?"

He nodded.

She started to turn away, but he caught her back and put his arms around her. She squeezed him in return and he heard her sniff, but when he released her, there wasn't a tear in sight. Who was the toughest of them all now?

The French toast had grown cold, so he scraped it into the trash and carefully rinsed his plate and placed it in the sink. He threw a glance at Mimi, who had settled with her coffee and a book as if she hadn't just chewed his ass from here to Sunday. Just another day at the Moon Ranch.

His lips quirked up on the corner as he walked over to drop a kiss on her cheek. "I'll be home for supper."

She reached up and patted the side of his face. "Don't do anything stupid."

"I'll try not to."

As he took care of Mimi's two chickens, he considered all that had been exchanged just now. He guessed he'd needed a good wakeup call, and Mimi had given it to him. But he still wasn't sure that Esme didn't deserve someone who could give her more than a stack of bills and a bleak future.

* * * * *

Just as he was headed to his truck, his phone rang. He pulled it out and stared at the screen a moment before putting it to his ear. "Moon."

"Didn't know if I had the right number. That batty woman you have up there on the ranch gave me your cell number, but I had no idea if she was speaking gibberish."

Fury coated his tongue, heavy and thick. "Who the fuck's this and what do you want?"

That someone would speak about Mimi that way took him beyond fury—he was already clenching his fists and looking for faces to ruin.

"Jefferson—up the road a few miles."

"I know the name. You were a rotten son of a bitch when I was a kid and it sounds like you got stupider. What the fuck do you want?"

"You never knew when to shut up, did ya, kid?"

He pictured the man, once tall and strong stock from ranchin'. But the man had to be pushin' his seventies by now, and Zayden could have taken him at seventeen.

"Why the hell are you calling me?" he barked into the phone.

"Your brother's here, passed out drunk on my lawn."

It wasn't the warmest of days. How long had he been there?

"You sure he's drunk?"

"Yeah, I know the smell of booze on a man. I remember your father well." Another dig. People like this made living in Stokes miserable — and also the reason he would never outrun hatred for the name Moon.

"I'll be up." Without waiting for a response, Zayden ended the call and jumped into his truck. He shot a look at the house, thinking of Mimi and what the woman might have endured while speaking to that asshole on the phone.

He glared out the window. Zayden would make him take back his words, nice and remorseful-like. He clamped his hands on the wheel, thinking of Jefferson's neck.

Squinting into the sun as he headed down the road, he tugged his hat low to shield his eyes. How had his brother ended up at the Jefferson place? He could only assume it was Dane — that he'd left the ranch and gone on a bender, driven drunk up to the wrong ranch and passed out on his way into the wrong house.

Lying in the cold Colorado weather wouldn't help out the brain cells he'd already burned through with alcohol. When Zayden got hold of him... Well, things wouldn't get any easier for his brother.

What a screwed up family. One would think that because of their father's alcoholism that the rest of the family would detest the stuff, but not Dane. While Zayden would smash bottles and dump 80-proof down drains, Dane would sneak sips as a teen.

It had led to him and Mimi sending Dane to a rehab at a young age, and he'd returned with a better outlook on life. Of course, that didn't last long in their household.

How many people you gonna fuck up, old man? he asked his father, wherever he was.

"Son of a bitch," he said to himself and turned into the drive leading to the Jeffersons'. Compared to the Moon Ranch, it looked like the President of the United States lived here, with miles of pristine fencing and every outbuilding sporting a new roof. There were too many horses in the pasture to count.

He wasn't looking for a horse—he was here for his brother.

He scoured the front lawn. Here at least some of the snow had burned off by the sun, and Dane was smart enough to pass out there.

As he drew to a stop, he saw the owner leave his barn and cross the yard. Ignoring him, Zayden went straight to his brother. He knelt in the soggy grass and grabbed Dane's shoulder. He was lying crumpled on one side, snoring deeply.

"Jesus, you reek." He shook Dane.

His head jostled boneless on his neck, and Zayden slapped him across the face.

He cracked an eye and said, "Wha — ?"

"You passed out in some rancher's yard and he wants you out."

Staring down at his brother, he couldn't dislike him more. Yet the urge to see him cared for was strong. He wasn't about to take him home and tuck him into bed, though. As far as he was concerned, Dane had chosen a path and could only walk it alone. Either he'd wake up wanting a better life for himself or he wouldn't.

The crunch of boots and the man approaching made Zayden raise his head. He threw up a hand to ward off the rancher. All he needed was for the guy to say a few more ugly things about his family and he'd be sitting in the Stokes jail.

"Dane, get up, man." His brother's hat lay in the grass, soaked. Zayden slapped it over his head, hoping the wet cold feel would startle him awake enough to get on his feet.

"Just like his pa," Jefferson said.

"Shut the hell up while you still got teeth." Zayden cast him a glower.

"You don't come onto my land and speak to me that way."

"Then go back inside and leave us be. I'll get my brother outta your hair." Zayden grabbed Dane by the shoulders and hauled him into a sitting position. He opened both eyes and started to topple to the side. Zayden caught him and held him there.

"Dane, look at me."

"Z?"

"Yeah, it's me. You need to get on your feet and into my truck."

He started to nod but made a grab for his head. "Too much...whiskey..."

"No shit. Come on. Get up now." He circled his brother's middle with his arms and hauled him up. He weighed more than a couple of calves, but he managed to get him onto his feet.

"Where's your truck? Didn't you drive here?" Zayden asked.

"Dunno how I got here."

He groaned. Someone had probably dropped him at the wrong ranch, which meant his truck was still at the bar.

His hat fell off, and Zayden released Dane to grab it. But his brother started to tip, and all he could do was get a shoulder beneath him and heave him over his back.

"Don't you dare fucking puke on me, man," he grated out.

"Don't come back," the rancher called out.

"We won't. Don't ever speak about Mimi that way again or you won't like waking in the night to find me hovering over you." Zayden strode across the yard, steps slowed by his brother's dead weight. When he got to the truck, he yanked the tailgate open and tossed his brother into the bed. Dane didn't wake from his stupor.

With a grunt of disgust, Zayden threw his wet hat in with him and slammed the gate closed.

He took the bumpy gravel drive fast, making sure to hit every pothole and rock he could. His brother bounced around in the back but didn't stir.

Hell, the last thing he needed was to take care of another drunk. He wouldn't stand for it. Dane had to go.

Hitting the road home, he stepped on the gas. A loud rap of knuckles on the window behind his head made him look around to see Dane sitting up. "Let me in!" he yelled and then clutched his head.

He slowed and pulled off. In the rearview mirror, he watched his brother climb out on unsteady legs and wobble to the passenger door. He slipped into the truck and eyed Zayden.

"I'm sorry. Victoria and I were fighting again. I told her I was comin' home to Vegas and she said don't expect to come home. All I could think to do was hit the bar."

Zayden shook his head. "You can't stick around here, man. I can't haul your ass out of someone's yard every morning after you've decided to get wasted. I won't take care of you like we had to with Dad."

"Don't blame ya. I'm not good to anyone, not even my wife."

He wanted to ask if the stripper was even worth fighting for, but held his tongue.

"Look, I've been thinkin' about that money you need—"

"I take it back. I don't need it." Zayden whipped the truck back out onto the road, making his brother rock against the door and groan.

"But what if I want part of the ranch?"

"I don't want to give it to someone who drowns his sorrows at the bottom of a bottle. I'll take you back to the bar for your truck. I suggest you sober up, sleep it off, before driving out."

"You're really kicking me out?"

"Yeah, I am. It's hard on me too, brother. I love ya…" His voice cracked. "But I won't have you around like this."

Dane remained silent the rest of the ride to the bar. Sure enough, his truck was there.

"I was headed out of town anyway," he said. "Guess I'll head back to Vegas. At least I've got a job and Victoria might take me back."

271

He didn't want to ask what he'd done to fall out of grace with her—her standards couldn't be all that high, so Zayden didn't want to know.

He brought the truck to a lurching stop just to be an asshole and was satisfied when Dane grabbed his stomach.

"Don't puke in my truck."

Dane popped the door and stumbled out. He stood there a moment, eyes bloodshot as he stared at Zayden. "I love ya too, brother. And don't worry—I'm not mad about this. I'll see ya again someday."

He started to shut the door, but Zayden called, "Wait!"

He paused. Zayden dug in his jeans pocket and came out with the AA token. He flipped it, and Dane missed the catch in his lower state of aptitude, but he picked it up off the truck seat and stared at it. "Yours?" he asked.

He shook his head. "Dad's. Maybe someday it will mean something to you and you'll do better than he did. Bye, Dane."

His brother closed the truck door and slowly walked to his own vehicle. Zayden's chest burned with anger at the situation. He couldn't help Dane—he'd fought that uphill battle enough as a kid. This was best.

But it hurt like hell.

It also made him realize he wasn't fooling himself or anyone else. He was a Moon—was no good and never would be.

While he drove into town, his mind fixed on Esme. So beautiful and with her whole life ahead of her. Going back to college to complete her degree, with ambitions of a promotion. Only problem with her was she was a bum magnet, and look at what she'd attracted—him.

All of the things he'd told her the previous night had to be forgotten. Mimi's words were pointless too. He had to break things off and stop trying to gain something he could never hold on to.

Chapter Fourteen

"That man is fiiine." The whispered words coming from Natalie made Esme peek around the customer she was serving. Shock rippled through her, along with a healthy dollop of desire, as she set eyes on Zayden.

In barn coat, boots and hat, he looked like walking sin as he strode through the lobby. He didn't bother knocking on Jason's door—he just swung it open, stepped inside and closed it.

Esme swallowed hard. Did his every action, even the bad-boy ones, have to be so hot? She smiled at her customer and finished the transaction, sending them off with a cheery goodbye.

The minute the woman left, Natalie scooted over to Esme. "Did you see the way he just walked into Jason's office like he owns it *and* the man?"

Esme drew in a shaky breath. After what she'd confided in Zayden the previous night, she had no idea if he might confront Jason and end things with his own flare.

And she hoped that didn't involve breaking his nose.

She quickly turned her attention to the customers entering the credit union. Jason's office door remained shut, and from here, she couldn't see Zayden at all through the glass window.

Her worry couldn't get the best of her—she had work to do. She focused all her energy on the customers' deposit and counting the bills correctly. When they left, there was another in line, and she took him too.

Customers continued to stream in and Zayden didn't come out. Suddenly, a male voice rose, loud enough to project through the walls of Jason's office, but it died down as fast as it had risen.

She pressed her lips together. What was going on in there? Was this about the loan or her? She suspected it could be both.

As she finished with the last customer of the small rush, the office door burst open. Zayden walked out—and he didn't even throw her a backward glance.

Her heart hit her chest wall hard. What the… She gripped the counter 'til her fingertips grew white.

How dare he act as if he didn't even know that she worked here. After all they'd shared last night… Pain and fury swelled inside her, too big to control.

She rounded the counter, pushed open the locked security door and took off after him. Behind her, she heard Natalie say, "What are you doing?"

But she ignored the question and shoved through the glass door leading outside. "Zayden!"

He stopped on the sidewalk but didn't turn. Damn him to hell.

Her high heels clacked as she rushed up to him and skirted his big body to face him down. With her hands on her hips, she tipped her head up to glare at him. "What was that about?"

"Just talkin' to the manager."

"You…stubborn…ass. That isn't what I mean, and you know it. What was that?" she demanded.

"Esme—"

"You think you can treat me that way after the things you said to me last night?"

His eyes darkened, but he dropped his stare and dipped his head, hiding under the brim of his hat.

She grabbed a fistful of his coat and stepped closer. "You are not doing this to me!"

"Esme, I don't want to talk about it here."

"Too bad—it's happening right here, right now. Is this your way of dumping me? The avoidance tactic? And here I thought you were the most man I'd ever had in my life, Zayden Moon."

That got a rise out of him. His jaw hardened, and his lips drew into a line. He didn't speak, though.

Frustration hit, and she couldn't bottle it up any longer. "What is this? Tell me! Say it."

"I thought I could do a relationship, but it's not me. I'm sorr—"

"Bullshit," she bit off through clenched teeth. "You started it and you're seeing it through. I won't let us *not happen* because of some false assumption by you that you can't handle it. Now look at me like you did last night and tell me those things again. Say you love me, so I stop wanting to punch you in the teeth."

His brows shot up. "What have I turned you into? Threatening me and making a scene in front of your workplace?"

She drew up, leveling her glare at him. "You aren't the only bad-ass in town, Moon. I may have some training to do on that front, but I'm determined to show the stubbornest man alive that what we mean to each other isn't a passing phase."

He stared at her, silent. Just when she thought he'd never speak to her again, he said, "I got my loan."

Some of her ire fizzled away. Nodding, she said, "I'm glad. You can use the money and fix up that ranch of yours, so you can stop being an ass about that portion of your life. Now, what are we doing to fix the relationship part?"

His Adam's apple bobbed in his throat. Her blood pressure was about to take another spike, but he reached out and brushed the curls back from her cheek. "God, I don't know what I did to deserve you."

"You did plenty, so shut up and quit wallowing in your past. Take charge of your future." She held out her hands, waiting for him to take them.

"I don't have anything to give you."

"That's a load of crap. You've got plenty, and we'll do it together. I'll help on the ranch as much as I can, but I'll be busy between work and night classes."

His eyes softened, but the muscle in the crease of his jaw fluttered. "You're hard to say no to."

"I learned from someone never to compromise when it comes to what I want." She chanced a smile at him.

When he slipped his hands into hers, tightened his hold and tugged her into his arms, a half-laugh, half-sob escaped her. She swallowed it down and pressed her cheek to his chest, over the layers of canvas and flannel he wore.

He brought his arms around her, holding her there a minute. "I'm sorry, sweetheart."

"You'll make it up to me."

He drew back to look into her eyes. "How?"

"You forget I know where you keep your rope."

A broad grin stretched across his handsome face. "Two women today have told me I'm a stupid ass."

She cocked a brow. "Mimi?"

He nodded.

"I knew I liked that woman."

He drew her back into his arms and buried his face against her hair. "Esme... Hell. You know I love you."

A shiver of emotion threaded through her, and she held him tight for a long moment, just breathing in his scent and knowing that together, they could tackle any trouble that came their way.

"You should go back inside. You've got work to do," he said.

She nodded. "I don't want to let you go."

"I'll be here. I'm not runnin'. I promise you, Esme."

Tears burned behind her eyes again. "I'll come to the ranch after work."

He leaned in and brushed his lips over hers, gently and too fleeting for her liking. But they stood in a public place, and for now it was enough. She kissed him back and started toward the entrance.

He grabbed her back, spinning her into his arms and pulling her off her feet. She clung to his neck, burning with love for him.

"Zayden—"

"I'm afraid you'll walk out on me." His quiet admission was her undoing.

A tear trickled down her face. "I keep my promises. Do you?" She eyed him.

He set her on her feet and nodded.

"Good. It's time to give Moon a good name in this town."

He shot a look over her head to the entrance.

"Oh no. I don't like that look on your face."

"I might have roughed up your manager a little bit."

"Zayden!"

"I couldn't help it. I signed the preliminary paperwork for them to do an appraisal and I got to thinkin' about that asshole treating you the way he did."

"Oh my God." She shook her head. Despite the man's sometimes illegal way of doing things, she couldn't help but love him for sticking up for her. "Don't do anything like that again!"

"Can't make promises I won't keep. But I'm pretty sure he won't bother you again. You'd best get back inside now." He cupped her face, and she leaned into his hand. "Come up tonight. We'll look in on the calf."

Heart warmed by his gaze and the bond the calf had created for them, she rubbed her cheek against his rough hand. "See you later."

He let her go and continued to his truck. She watched him get in and reverse from the spot. At the last minute before leaving the parking lot, he tipped his hat to her in farewell, and she swiped away another tear, this one of happiness.

* * * * *

"Z?" Mimi called out to him as he entered the house.

"Yeah. I got the mail." He transferred it to one hand as he shook off the sleeve of his jacket and then hung it up. When he walked in, he found Mimi on a ladder, a small paint bucket balanced in one hand and a brush in the other. Pale blue paint created a stripe between ceiling and wall as she trimmed out the living room.

"What in the world?" he asked, looking up at her.

"I figured it's about time this place looks brighter." She looked up at the blue. "What do you think of the color?"

"I think you made the perfect choice. It's the same blue as the sky today—and your eyes too."

"Flatterer. Always were." She eyed him. "You take care of things with your girl?"

He scuffed his boot on the worn carpet. "I tried to screw things up again, but she wouldn't let me."

"Good. Knew she was strong enough to keep the likes of you in line. I'm coming down and we'll have a look at that mail."

He nodded and watched her set the plastic bucket on the tray ledge and descend to the floor. She took the mail out of his hands and walked into the kitchen. He went for coffee, which was still hot, and poured a mug while she sorted the mail.

"Junk. More junk. This one's from the sheriff's office, addressed to you."

"I'll take that." He held out his hand, but she looked straight at him and slit the envelope with her fingertip.

As she began to skim-read the letter, he brought his coffee to his lips. "Ya know, it's a federal offense to open someone else's mail," he drawled.

She shook her head. "Says here, your fine's been doubled for late payment." She read on and then lifted her head. "Public urination. Well, I hope that piss was worth four-hundred-fifty dollars."

"It was." He thought of that asshole deputy he'd gone to school with and wouldn't do a thing different.

She sighed and set the letter aside, going for another. "This is addressed to you too. Community service? When did you have time for all this mischief, Zayden?"

He chuckled. "I'll chop some wood for the sheriff or somethin'. Don't worry—I'll take care of it."

Another envelope. "This here's the vet bill."

That brought a heavy sigh from him. "I'll take care of that too."

"Don't forget about that fifteen grand you need to buy back the horses."

"Or the ten I owe the coalition for that loan." None of this was news to him—he knew he had obligations and a bunch of bills to settle.

She tossed aside a feed catalog to read later and picked up another envelope. Her brows knitted as she read the front. "This looks like…" She blinked rapidly and tore into the envelope. "It is."

He set down his coffee and moved toward her. "It is what?"

"It's in Dane's handwriting. But it wasn't mailed. There's no postage. He must have put it into the mailbox before he left town."

Zayden's heart flexed hard. "Give it to me."

She handed the envelope to him and watched as he pulled the contents free. When his gaze hit a check addressed to him with a fifteen and a three zeroes following the number, a rough sigh escaped his lungs.

Mimi hovered over his arm to read the check and then plastered a hand over her chest. "My Lord. Your brother didn't leave you high and dry, after all, did he?"

He swallowed the lump in his throat. "No…" A small scribbled note sat nestled against the check.

Brother, hope this helps and keeps some of my cut of the ranch. I have a feeling I'll be needing a home soon. And don't worry – I won't come back just to act like Dad.
    –Dane

He pinched the bridge of his nose hard. "Damn," he said softly.

Mimi patted his arm, beaming through her tears. "That buys back those horses your dad stole. Which reminds me that Jefferson called for you earlier. What a terrible jerk that man is."

"Yeah," seemed to be the word to cover all those topics. His voice came out gritty.

"Now about that fine for peeing in public—"

He held up a hand against the lecture. "I said I'll take care of it."

"I know you will—you're honorable. I was just gonna add that you handled all this very well today." She squeezed his arm. "You've grown a lot since coming home, Z."

To cover his emotion raised by her words, he withdrew his wallet and put the check inside. Then he stuffed the note in as well, suddenly unwilling to throw away even a small scrap of paper from his brother. For a moment, he stood there in shock that so many pieces were falling into place.

The loan was going through and soon he'd have his money. His brother just saved his ass with the check that would cover some of the mess his father left behind. Mimi still had his back, and he couldn't be more grateful for her.

And Esme too.

He needed to make it up to her for trying to walk out without speaking today. What had gotten into him, anyway? His mind was like a wild stallion sometimes, taking off alone to live a solitary existence, when all it wanted really was a warm stall and a bucket of hay. Only thing he could say for certain was Esme deserved better—but if she wanted him, then he'd do his best.

Swallowing hard again, he returned his wallet to his pocket and turned to Mimi. "I've got some things to take care of."

She nodded. "I'll see you for supper?"

"Yeah. Esme too. She'll be here."

Mimi gave him a knowing smile. "Can't wait to see her again."

As he walked out to the barn to check on the new addition to the Moon Ranch, he couldn't help but wait for the other shoe to drop—to find another mess from his father or discover that he really was the biggest dick of all the Moons and Esme couldn't abide being with him.

He paused in the yard and tipped his face up to the sky.

Whatever happened, he had himself—and he could always rely on that. He wasn't his father, a drunk or conniving thief. He might not always take the high road, but that didn't make him a bad man...and he had every chance to make things right.

Starting now, he was going to live on his terms, without the shadow of his upbringing hanging like a dark cloud over his head.

* * * * *

"Mimi?" Esme poked her head into the kitchen. "Is Zayden around?"

The woman turned from a basket of laundry to smile at her. "He's in the barn." A twinkle in her eyes made her suspicious as to what the woman knew that she didn't.

"I'll come back in to talk to you later, then." She smiled and headed back outside.

Long shadows of evening stretched across the thawing ground, and she tracked them with her eyes as she made her way to the barn. When she laid a hand on the wood door, she paused.

He was inside, and she couldn't wait to see him. But part of her was apprehensive too. After he'd tried to end their relationship, she had no idea what side of Zayden to expect.

Time to find out.

She pushed open the door. The scent of hay rose up to greet her, and she blinked at a yellow circle of light coming from a lantern along one wall. On the floor beneath that, a blanket was spread out and several more folded and set aside. Next to that sat a picnic basket.

"What the..." She stepped closer, and then a strong arm came around her middle. The feel of the man behind her had her body on high alert. His scent rushed into her head as he dipped his mouth to her ear.

"Surprise." His murmur raised the hairs all over her body.

"What is this?" she asked, turning into his arms.

He brought her close. "It's me making up to you. And since I only know women like romantic picnics, I had Mimi help me out."

It was too cold outside for such a thing, and the fact that he'd brought it into the barn was the sweetest thing she'd ever heard.

"I cleaned the barn real good first."

She smiled up at him. "It's perfect. Zayden…" There weren't words for what she felt, so she went on tiptoe and kissed him.

The soft brushing of lips spoke of promises untold. But in time, she'd get each and every one from this man. He wasn't as tough as he looked — or acted. And he was hers.

She broke the kiss and rested her forehead against his, breathing hard.

"What do you want to do first? Eat or see the calf?" He tipped his head toward the far stall where he had the mother and baby tucked up warm and safe.

"See the calf. I've been wondering about it all day." She stepped back, and he caught her hand. They shared a long look before he led her to the stall and opened the door.

The momma looked up at them, munching hay while the baby nestled next to her side, nursing.

"She's on her feet!" Esme exclaimed.

"Yeah, happens pretty quick."

"She's adorable. I can't believe I helped her be born."

Zayden's stare was a warm weight on her, and she met it. Electric desire passed between them.

He closed the stall and took her hand again. This time he drew her toward the glow at the other side of the barn.

He waved a hand for her to sit on the blanket, and she did. Her coat was bulky but necessary — at least till he started touching her. Then she'd warm pretty quick.

Looking a bit nervous, Zayden sank to the blanket as well. She wondered if he'd ever had a picnic in his life.

"What have we got to eat?" She leaned to peer at the basket.

He popped open the wood lid and reached inside. "Tea." The plastic jug was set aside, along with a couple mugs. "Chicken." He set aside a small container. "And biscuits."

"Mmm."

"And for dessert —"

She threw herself forward to kiss the words off his lips. When he sank his tongue into her mouth, she moaned and deepened the caress. Passion was a wick inside her caught aflame by Zayden's lips and tongue.

As he dragged her into his lap, she threw off the coat she wore and wrapped her arms around his neck.

He moved her so she straddled him. The hard bulge in his jeans nudged at her center, and in seconds they were both panting for more.

"Dinner can wait," she muttered between passes of his tongue.

"Dessert first." He captured her lips and stole all thought of food from her mind. All she wanted was to taste this cowboy, feel his callused hands stripping her... and then his thick cock pounding into her.

He had the same idea. Cupping her breasts, he moved to kiss her neck. Dizzying seconds passed, and before she knew it, his hands were on bare skin, her top discarded.

He dragged the work-rough pads of his thumbs across her nipples, and she sucked in a sharp breath. He kissed her open mouth, tongue swirling with hers in the deepest of kisses as he laid her down. To her surprise, the blanket rested on a bed of hay. She wrapped her arms around his broad shoulders and drew him closer.

"This is perfect," she whispered.

He searched her eyes. "You're perfect."

Her heart flip-flopped with another injection of love. When she'd been stranded and alone on that mountain, she never would have believed this was in store for her. That she'd have someone as noble and strong as Zayden in her life was still a shock. And their fledgling friendship—and his protectiveness of her—had morphed into so much more.

She tangled her fingers in the hair on his nape and took pleasure in the rasp of his stubbled jaw against her skin. He moved down to her throat, then her breasts and continued on.

She fumbled off his shirt and skated her hands over all his warm flesh. The chiseled bumps fed into her desire, and the glow of lantern light carved him out of stone. She kissed every inch she could reach, and he did the same. When he stripped off her dress pants and then his own jeans followed, they stared at each other.

"I'm shaking," she whispered.

He clenched his hands into fists. "You're so goddamn beautiful."

She arched her back, pushing her breasts forward. The hard peaks begged for his lips and teeth. "Are you gonna tie me up again?"

His eyes burned. "You liked that, did you?"

She nodded, hardly able to catch her breath let alone form words. "It was more than sex."

"I know." His gritty tone had her nipples pinching harder. Then things got fuzzy, as his mouth enveloped one tip and she stopped thinking.

Reaching between their bodies, she cupped his cock—hard and turgid, the head swollen and slick with pre-cum. She moaned and enveloped him with her fingers. Stroking up and down his length, she drew groan after wild groan from him. He dropped his head against her neck and let her have her way for several long heartbeats before he grabbed her wrist.

"Let me taste you," she rasped.

He gave a rough shake of his head. "Can't hold back if you do. I want you too much, sweetheart." He rolled onto his back and grasped her by the hips. "Straddle my face."

Dark heat slithered through her belly at the idea of his mouth hitting her wet folds. With a quiet mewl of desire, she eased her thighs on each side of his ears. Hot breath washed across her pussy.

He cupped her ass cheeks and dragged her down to meet his lips.

* * * * *

He'd never played the seduction game, but he couldn't help planning out more scenarios for him and Esme in his mind. By the time he had her sitting on his face, he'd made a mental list to execute and had her squirming atop him all at once.

She tossed back her head on a cry, and he sucked her tight bud into his mouth, flickering his tongue across the bundle of nerves till she quaked. Her delicious flavors flooded over his lips, and he eased a finger between her cheeks, down to her dripping pussy.

When he dipped the tip into her channel, she thrashed. He held on, sinking his finger deeper into

291

her pussy as he sucked her clit. His cock ached and his balls throbbed. If he lasted through this moment, he had more stamina than he thought.

Hell, I'm a Moon. If nothing else, I can pleasure a woman and keep her coming back for more.

He never wanted this woman to leave his bed. Or his side. With her, the future wasn't all storm clouds and trouble on the horizon. He could see the sun through the storm.

As this poetry passed through his mind, he pulsed his finger faster. He gathered her juices and sucked her clit between his lips. The moment she tightened on his finger, he added a second and brought a wail from her lips.

She came hard, churning her hips, ass grinding and taking everything she needed from him. A heady power unlike anything he'd known before stole his mind, and he lifted her, flipped her onto her back, and got a condom from the stash he'd placed under the blankets.

Their gazes locked, he took her in one hard thrust. When the haze of passion in her eyes was too much for him to endure, he began to move.

Their harsh noises filled the barn, and he couldn't think of anywhere else he'd want to be right now than buried deep inside Esme. She stared into his eyes and kissed him with the wildness he needed to tip him over the edge. She wasn't ready for a second orgasm yet, but it was too late—he couldn't stop it.

Sensation rushed up from the base of his spine, a tingling that erupted on a wave. He growled low in his throat, and she gripped him to her as the release struck.

When she raked her fingertips down his spine, another jet pulsed out of his cock, and another. Someday he'd have her without barriers, and that day would come soon.

'Til then, there was always rope.

* * * * *

"There's a new vet in town." Mimi's announcement had him stopping midstride to the front door.

He half-turned. "Maybe this one doesn't know our bad reputation."

Mimi laughed at that. "Or maybe you finally paid off the other and she skipped town before you could rope her into more work here."

He chuckled. "That too."

"Where are you headed?" she asked.

He shot her a crooked grin. "To do my community service." He'd agreed to cut down bushes outside the sheriff's office and come spring thaw, he'd dig out the roots for new plantings. He had a feeling the decision to make him dig up the roots was all Dickies' idea, but he wasn't about to argue. Things were going too well to let that old rival get to him.

Mimi bustled over to put her arms around him. She gave him a fat kiss on the cheek and he rubbed it away, like he did when he was thirteen.

"Ew."

She laughed. "I'm going to start painting the kitchen next."

He nodded. "Want me to pick up some paint in town?"

"If you wouldn't mind stopping by the hardware store, I have a paint chip selected. Let me get it."

He looked around the living room while she fetched the paint chip. Funny how a coat of paint changed things. The blue was brighter and pale enough to look like clouds. As soon as he got back from the cattle auction with some more stock, he'd budget out a new floor in here. Maybe hardwood if the used tractor he planned to buy didn't cost that much.

She returned with a smile and put the chip into his hand.

"It's just white," he said.

"It's farmhouse ivory. Not white."

He shrugged. "I'll pick some up. Be home for supper."

"Bring Esme."

He grinned. "I will."

The work cutting down shrubs lasted all afternoon, and he felt grubby and his muscles burned from all the hard work. He had a few more days on the job, but at least he could say he dug himself out of trouble at the same time. Maybe a Moon could learn from his mistakes, after all.

He just passed the steakhouse on his way to the hardware store, when he spotted Esme's car.

His heart gave a hard jolt. Why had she come here so late in the day? Hell, lunchtime had just passed.

Unusual for her to buy such a pricey lunch. Who could she be with?

Trust her. Drive past and buy the paint.

He couldn't do that. What if she got in over her head? Last time she'd come here, she'd met that idiot ex who'd dumped her on the mountain.

He whipped into the parking lot.

With measured strides, he stormed into the building and looked around for her curls.

"Can I seat you, sir?" the hostess asked.

He shook his head. "Lookin' for someone." When he spotted her mop of hair, his throat closed off.

She sat alone.

He took off toward her, weaving through tables till he reached one near the window. Esme sat looking out, her chin propped on the heel of her hand.

"What are you doin' here?" he asked unceremoniously.

She jerked and blinked up at him in shock. "Zayden."

"Are you meeting somebody?"

She shook her head and then smiled softly. "Sit down."

Chest tight with confusion, he dropped to the wooden chair. "What's going on?"

"I was celebrating."

His jaw dropped. "Celebrating what?" Without him?

She folded her hands on the table. "My promotion."

He gaped at her. "Promotion? I thought that jerk-off wasn't giving it to you without a degree."

"It seems that I'm the best candidate for the position. He's interviewed about a dozen people, and since I know the credit union policies already and I am currently attending classes to complete my degree... Well, it wasn't only Jason's decision, anyway. The president of the credit union came today and told us all that I'm the new loan officer."

He issued a breath of relief, and on the heels of that came a whoop of happiness.

The few people enjoying the lunch menu looked over at them, but what did he care about a little attention when his woman had gone after her own dream and attained it?

She grinned at him and reached out to take his hands. Her touch jarred him back to his darker thoughts.

"You were celebrating without me," he said flatly.

Her face fell. "No. Well, yes. I thought I deserved to treat myself to a good lunch, and I knew you were doing your…thing at the sheriff's office today. I couldn't call you to come join me. But I did have other plans to celebrate with you tonight." Her eyes twinkled, and he could guess what by the way she bit down on her plump lower lip.

His cock stirred at the sight, his heart full of happiness for her. His own life was better because of Esme. *He* was better.

He couldn't let her go.

He wanted her.

He slid out of the chair and dropped to one knee.

Esme stared at him. He looked into her beautiful eyes and knew this was all he wanted for himself for the rest of his life.

"Zayden…"

"Esme…"

"You fool, get up!"

He shook his head. "I'm not so much of a fool that I'll let another day pass without asking you to walk through life with me." He took her hand and rubbed his thumb over her knuckles.

"This isn't necessary. It's crazy, Z."

He gave her a crooked grin. "You knew I was crazy when you took up with me. But I'm dead serious right now, sweetheart. I love you and I won't leave without trying to convince you to be my wife."

Her lips parted on a sigh that made no noise.

"Fuck, I don't have a ring yet, but sweetheart, first thing in the morning I will get you one if you'll marry me."

* * * * *

If she could breathe, she might be able to think straight. If she could process what Zayden was saying to her... But she watched his lips moving and heard words coming from his mouth that she never thought to hear, let alone so soon.

He was seriously on bended knee proposing to her in the middle of the steakhouse. Her throat clogged off, and she focused on the callus of his thumb moving across her fingers.

One of the things he'd said lit a bulb in her mind.

A laugh-cry escaped her. "How will you get a ring without money? Who will you sweet-talk or rough up to get it?"

"I have my ways..." His grin widened, 'til all she could see was the gorgeous man in front of her, telling her he would love her for the rest of his days.

"Esme. Sweetheart. Just say yes and we'll figure out the rest." His gaze burned through her. "Please. I love you with everything in me."

The love words couldn't have been better said if they'd come from a love ballad or poet. They were true—they were pure Zayden.

A cry escaped her, and she slipped off the chair into his waiting arms. Throwing hers around his neck, she clung to him. "Yes! You crazy cowboy. I love you!"

He claimed her lips, and applause broke out around them. As Zayden kissed her to seal their promise to each other, she shook with emotion.

The day that had begun as great, following the surprise news of her promotion, had transformed to a quiet moment eating alone reflecting on how far she'd come in this world. And the thing that surfaced highest on the list of joys was Zayden. She didn't want to let him go—wanted to share everything with him. She'd just been wishing he would join her to celebrate when he showed up.

Now he was her fiancé.

He pulled back from the kiss and stared into her eyes. "I promise you'll never regret it, sweetheart."

She squeezed him tighter. "I know I won't."

Another round of applause sounded, and both of them realized they had an audience. He stood and drew her to her feet too. They linked hands and looked at the few patrons in the restaurant who were staring with their meals forgotten. Even the dishwasher had wandered out of the kitchen to witness the proposal.

"We've got something else to celebrate now, sweetheart. I'm dirty from working all morning, and Mimi expects me back with some paint for the kitchen, but let's sit down together and have that steak dinner we never had months ago."

Tears filled her eyes, and she blinked them away so she could see the hunky man before her. As they took their seats, he captured her hands and held them while he looked into her eyes.

"You've made me the happiest man on Earth. I never thought... Well, I never thought I'd feel this way about a woman or my life." His words grated across her senses, flooding her with the need to be in his arms again.

That would come soon enough. She didn't think they'd make it back to the Moon Ranch before stopping off to make love on some back road.

"I'm so happy, Zayden. I love you."

His smile was the only answer she ever needed. Making him happy had become a priority in her life, just as her own happiness had long ago become his.

He squeezed her fingers. "You'd better call in and say you won't be returning to work this afternoon."

She giggled. "Doesn't exactly look good when I was just promoted."

"You were also just engaged."

300

She nodded. "I'll call off on one condition."

He arched a brow. "What's that?"

Under the table, she slid the toe of her high heel up his calf.

His gaze intensified. "Oh yeah." He pitched his voice low. "I won't let you out of bed for a lonnnng time, sweetheart."

"That's the promise I wanted to hear."

Epilogue

"Babe..."

Zayden looked up from sliding on his boots to see his woman braced in the bathroom doorway, looking very well loved and wearing nothing but a pair of skimpy panties.

His gut burned at the sight of her. Hell, she was tormenting him these past few months—he couldn't get enough of her.

She padded across the bedroom and wedged herself between his thighs. Dropping his boot, he put his hands on her bare waist. She leaned into him, and he tumbled her back into the sheets, where she lay staring up at him with come-hither eyes.

"Do you have to check the herd right now?"

He sighed. "Yeah. I do."

She trailed a fingertip down her breast, over the hard peak. He groaned and buried his face between them. Maybe the herd didn't need checking right now. Maybe they could wait another hour.

"You'd better go then. Hurry back, though, and maybe I'll still be lying here naked, waiting for you."

With extreme effort, he lifted his head from her sweet, fragrant breasts. "Give me half hour."

A soft smile lit her face, and she nodded. After one more squeeze, she released him. He didn't get up immediately, and she slapped his backside.

"Go on, cowboy. Check your animals and then come back to bed."

It was early—dawn wasn't even kissing the sky yet, and only a sliver of dark blue was visible on the horizon. But by the time he did his chores and made sure the fifty new head of cattle he'd purchased were well, the sun would be up. After that, going back to bed for a spell seemed the perfect way to spend a Saturday.

He pressed her curls away so he could kiss her. "Go back to sleep, sweetheart. I won't be long."

Her eyelids were already drifting shut. He left her curled on her side under the blankets and walked out of the house into the cool morning. The scent of fall was in the air, and he drew in a deep breath of it.

As he crossed the yard to the barn, he felt the familiar rush of love for the ranch he had every day since getting on his feet. He wouldn't call things perfect yet, but he was making headway. What debts he knew of were paid, he'd returned the horses to the owner and purchased cattle and a few new horses to help in his day-to-day work.

And Esme was his everything. Odd, that notion, but true. He'd never be perfect, but he slowly learned how to be there for her... To be the man she needed. Together, they had spent hours making plans for the Moon Ranch. She had a good head for the figures, and he gave her control of the budget while he made the executive decisions on how to get the most bang for their buck.

She had completed some classes already during the summer and enrolled in more. The hours taken from him for work and schooling would be well worth it someday, but he sure missed her when they were apart.

He thought of her asking him to stay in bed with her, and his stomach warmed. Seemed she missed being with him just as much. Yeah, life was good. If he fell down and turned up his toes right now, he would die a happy man.

Holy shit. I broke the cycle.

His stride faltered as he realized this. His father had most likely died miserable. When he'd knocked on death's door, none of his family was around him, and nobody was here to hold his hand as he let go. Zayden had vowed never to follow in the old man's footsteps, and dammit, he'd kept his promise to himself.

Inside the barn, he patted Zeus's side as he drew him out of the stall. "Hey, boy. Ready to ride?"

The horse responded with a low whicker. He led the animal into the yard and walked him a few times to work out the kinks. Then he saddled up and rode out to check the herd.

The solitude of the morning ride filled him with a peace he had never expected to achieve. When he spotted his cattle grazing in the distance, he spurred Zeus faster, eager to reach them.

With the land and two great women at his back, he could do anything, and dammit, he was going to make the Moon Ranch great.

After a thorough check of the herd, he headed back home, thinking of warm, silky skin and dark shadows between plump thighs…

In the newly painted kitchen, Mimi had the coffee going but was nowhere around. He heard the shower running and knew before long she'd be calling him and Esme to have breakfast.

Right now, though, he was keeping his promise to crawl back into bed with his beautiful, sexy, and needy woman.

He shed his boots before he reached the bedroom. When he opened the door, she was unmoving, eyes closed. His heart gave a hard squeeze as love swelled the organ even bigger than it already was.

As he moved toward the bed, he shucked his shirt and shoved off his jeans. His underwear and socks were last, and he slipped under the covers, bare flesh against her bare flesh.

Suddenly, she twisted into his arms and ran her hands over his chest. "That was fast."

"Told ya it wouldn't take long. Now where did we leave off?" He claimed her lips, kissing softly at first and then deepening it with tongues and soft moans. When he drew back, she caught his wrist and looped something around it.

He shook back the covers to see she held the end of the rope she'd bound around his wrist.

"Time for a little Saturday morning fun." She gripped his other hand and guided it toward the rope so she could fasten them together. Without hands, he couldn't touch her, and no way was that happening, even if the prospect of being at her mercy for a short time was highly exciting.

"Esme... Sweetheart, what are you doing?" he asked the obvious.

She bit her lip and attempted to tie him up. In a blink, he had her on her back, sprawled beneath him, arms stretched over her head.

"Not so fast. First I get my way with you." He did a slow pushup, brushing his body against her soft, feminine one. She moaned.

Wrapping her arms around his neck, she pulled him down. "Don't stop now."

He angled into her pussy. In one hard thrust, he joined them. The sensation of being bare inside her would never get old. He ground his hips, rubbing her deeper.

"Kiss me." Her rasped cry filled him with all the passion and love he'd never believed he deserved. How amazing that life had made a complete turn in such a short time. Only months ago, he was burying his father and feeling like letting this all go. Then he'd found Esme on that mountain, and he'd started to see a future.

Her gentle kisses turned hotter, and he plunged into her faster. They galloped toward the finish and when she finally cried out and shuddered beneath him, he let go, filling her with his seed that someday, when they were ready, would make a child.

With his face buried against her neck, he moaned. "I love you, sweetheart. Don't ever forget it."

She cupped his face and drew his head up to look into his eyes. "I could never forget, not when you show me every day of your life."

He rocked his hips once more, raising a groan from both of them. He collapsed onto the bed and drew her against his side while sliding a hand beneath the sheets.

She jerked. "Zayden!"

He caught her other hand and bound it to the first. Pinning both rope-knotted hands over her head, he slid down her body. "Spread your legs for me, baby. I'm going to taste both of us on you…"

Whatever she was about to say was swallowed on a gasp.

THE END

Read on for a SNEAK PEEK of SCREWED AND SATISFIED, the next book featuring the Moon boys.

The vase whizzed past Dane's head and struck the wall with an ear-splitting crack. Glass exploded, raining down on the carpet and mingling with the two broken beer bottles that landed there first.

Dane ducked yet another hurled object, this one with a trajectory hell-bent on taking off his head. "Calm down, Liz! Jesus, you know I like to unwind after work. It's not like I was in bed with another woman."

"Isn't sitting at the craps table all night long worse than sleeping with another woman? You lost our rent money—and next month's too. You told me if I came back to you that you wouldn't gamble anymore."

"You've seriously got your priorities mixed up if you don't give a damn if I'm cheatin', but you don't want me gamblin'." He eyed his wife. Her blonde hair trailed down into one eye, which blazed with anger.

"You can get pussy for free—but you owe those loan sharks how much now?"

He waved a hand, scoffing off her words. "I can make that back in two nights of dancin'. I'll let my thong slip and the ladies will toss enough twenties at me onstage to pay what I owe plus give us extra for that helicopter ride over the city you've always wanted to go on, baby."

Starting across the living room toward her, he held out a hand.

She picked up an ashtray and cocked her arm to hurl it too.

He clenched his jaw. "Put it down, Liz."

"Or what? You'll leave? If you ain't, I am! I never should have come back to you that third time. Or the fourth, for that matter."

He stared at his wife and tried to remember what it was about her had drawn him to her. Married a year and split every few months, he couldn't remember much.

"You know I never cheated on you," he said, low.

"Nah, you were too busy fondling your dice."

"Stay."

"Fuck you." She rifled the ashtray. The butts she smoked scattered and ashes cast out in a cloud. The jagged heavy glass blasted into the wall right where his head had been a moment before he ducked.

"Those guys have cornered me twice at work now. I can't have people coming to my workplace and demanding I pay them what you gambled away the night before, Dane. I'm leaving, and this time I want a divorce."

Her chest heaved, and the red mottling her face and throat turned him on. Always had. He loved when she got ticked at him, because it meant they could make up.

This time, though, he knew things had gone too far. *He'd* gone too far.

She thought the pennies he owed those guys who hassled her at the strip club where she worked was bad. Well, she hadn't discovered the fifteen grand missing from their bank account yet—the money he'd given his brother to help with the family's failing ranch.

Pushing out a sigh, he rubbed a hand over his tired face. Why did Liz have to get on his case right now? After a double shift at the club where he ground his hips to pop songs and changed out costumes—the firefighter had always been his favorite—he'd hit the casino and lost another grand.

"You've got a problem, Dane Moon." She twisted away from him and started grabbing any item that belonged to her. When she stomped into the bedroom, he followed, even though what he wanted to do was lie down on the couch and sleep.

"Baby. Lizzie. You know I love ya. I can't live without ya."

She cast him a dark look as she dropped the items on the bed and yanked out her suitcase that hadn't even been put away after the last time she left. As she packed it haphazardly with clothes and shoes, he stood there watching.

Did he really want her to leave?

Did he really want her to stay?

Maybe he should go. He hated Vegas. Hell, he'd only ended up here to get far away from the Moon Ranch and his drunken asshole of a father. Now with the man gone and his brother in charge, Dane could leave all this behind—his gig as a dancer in the male revue, drinking and gambling with people he'd never in a million years consider friends, the shabby apartment over a cigar shop he shared with a wife he couldn't remember why he married in the first place.

Or why he wanted her to stay, either.

"Go on and leave." He zipped up her bag for her while she dug another out from under the bed.

"I will!" Her breasts jiggled with each move she made, and he found one of the reasons he'd wanted her didn't look so appetizing these days. Liz had a bangin' body, that was true, but she knew how to use it on every single man in Vegas. The fact he didn't give a damn who she slept with woke him up further.

"You'd better take care of those loan sharks too. I don't want them coming after me again, Dane." She folded a knee-high glittery boot and stuffed it into the bag.

"I said I'll take care of them," he bit off. "Just send the divorce papers to the ranch."

"I fucking will!" With two bags stuffed to overflowing with her things, she grabbed one and slung the other over her shoulder. He watched her walk out and didn't make a move to stop her.

Buy Screwed and Satisfied at Amazon

Em Petrova

Em Petrova was raised by hippies in the wilds of Pennsylvania but told her parents at the age of four she wanted to be a gypsy when she grew up. She has a soft spot for babies, puppies and 90s Grunge music and believes in Bigfoot and aliens. She started writing at the age of twelve and prides herself on making her characters larger than life and her sex scenes hotter than hot.

She burst into the world of publishing in 2010 after having five beautiful bambinos and figuring they were old enough to get their own snacks while she pounds away at the keys. In her not-so-spare time, she is fur-mommy to a Labradoodle named Daisy Hasselhoff.

Find More Books by Em Petrova at empetrova.com

Other Titles by Em Petrova

Moon Ranch
TOUGH AND TAMED

313

SCREWED AND SATISFIED
CHISELED AND CLAIMED

Ranger Ops
AT CLOSE RANGE
WITHIN RANGE
POINT BLANK RANGE
RANGE OF MOTION
TARGET IN RANGE
OUT OF RANGE

Knight Ops Series
ALL KNIGHTER
HEAT OF THE KNIGHT
HOT LOUISIANA KNIGHT
AFTER MIDKNIGHT
KNIGHT SHIFT
ANGEL OF THE KNIGHT
O CHRISTMAS KNIGHT

Wild West Series
SOMETHING ABOUT A LAWMAN
SOMETHING ABOUT A SHERIFF
SOMETHING ABOUT A BOUNTY HUNTER
SOMETHING ABOUT A MOUNTAIN MAN

RYDER
RIDGE
WEST
LANE
WYNONNA

Rope 'n Ride On Series
JINGLE BOOTS
DOUBLE DIPPIN
LICKS AND PROMISES
A COWBOY FOR CHRISTMAS
LIPSTICK 'N LEAD

The Dalton Boys
COWBOY CRAZY Hank's story
COWBOY BARGAIN Cash's story
COWBOY CRUSHIN' Witt's story
COWBOY SECRET Beck's story
COWBOY RUSH Kade's Story
COWBOY MISTLETOE a Christmas novella
COWBOY FLIRTATION Ford's story
COWBOY TEMPTATION Easton's story
COWBOY SURPRISE Justus's story
COWGIRL DREAMER Gracie's story
COWGIRL MIRACLE Jessamine's story
COWGIRL HEART Kezziah's story

Single Titles and Boxes
STRANDED AND STRADDLED
LASSO MY HEART
SINFUL HEARTS
BLOWN DOWN
FALLEN
FEVERED HEARTS
WRONG SIDE OF LOVE

Club Ties Series
LOVE TIES
HEART TIES
MARKED AS HIS
SOUL TIES
ACE'S WILD

Firehouse 5 Series
ONE FIERY NIGHT
CONTROLLED BURN
SMOLDERING HEARTS

The Quick and the Hot Series
DALLAS NIGHTS
SLICK RIDER
SPURRED ON

EM PETROVA
WWW.EMPETROVA.COM

Made in the USA
Las Vegas, NV
25 May 2022

49352774R00177